*To my kids.*
*They voted for this book*
*a long time ago.*
*Sorry it took so long!*

# RUN

## DAVID SKUY

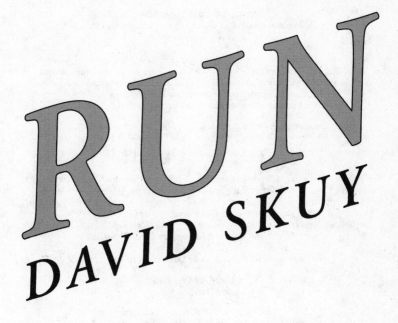

Canada Council
for the Arts
Conseil des Arts
du Canada
 ONTARIO ARTS COUNCIL
CONSEIL DES ARTS DE L'ONTARIO

Canadian    Patrimoine
Heritage    canadien
Canadä

The publisher gratefully acknowledges the support of the Canada Council for the Arts
and the Ontario Arts Council for its publishing program. We acknowledge the
financial support of the Government of Canada through the Canada Book Fund (CBF)
for our publishing activities, and the Government of Ontario through the Ontario
Media Development Corporation, an agency of the Ontario Ministry of Culture,
and the Ontario Book Publishing Tax Credit Program.

LIBRARY AND ARCHIVES CANADA CATALOGUING IN PUBLICATION

Skuy, David, 1963–, author
Run / David Skuy.

Issued in print and electronic formats.
ISBN 978-1-77086-488-7 (paperback).— ISBN 978-1-77086-489-4 (html)

I. Title.

PS8637.K72R86 2017        JC813'.6        C2016-907294-0
C2016-907295-9

Library of Congress Control Number: 2016945420

Cover design: angeljohnguerra.com
Interior text design: Tannice Goddard, bookstopress.com
Manufactured by Friesens in Altona, Manitoba, Canada in March, 2017.

Printed and bound in Canada.

CORMORANT BOOKS INC.
10 ST. MARY STREET, SUITE 615, TORONTO, ONTARIO, M4Y 1P9
www.cormorantbooks.com

## Wednesday: 8:50 a.m.

Lionel closed his eyes. His head began to pound, right at the base, and his chest ached, like someone was pressing on it, but slowly. He didn't dare let them notice, not for a second. If they saw his fear, sensed weakness, they'd pounce.

"Yo, Nick, I'm so open it hurts," Bryan yelled.

Nick hurled the football, a tight spiral. Bryan jumped. The ball bounced off his hands.

"Great catch, loser. Try catching it with your butt next time," Nick said.

"Try not throwing it over my head, moron," Bryan said.

He reached for the ball.

"I'll show you how it's done," Mohamed said, cutting across the school yard.

Bryan threw it. The ball wobbled, but Mohamed changed directions and scooped it up before it hit the asphalt.

Lionel glanced at the doors, anxious for the morning bell to ring. If he left school grounds, he might be late again. Principal Ryder was all over him lately. She'd even threatened to call his mom if he was late one more time. He pressed his back against the chain-link fence. At least at recess or lunch he could slip into a washroom stall, or the library, or head to the park.

Two boys, one blond with a round, soft face and freckles, and the other, short with brown hair and a backpack too big for his little frame, walked towards him. His heart began pounding. He didn't need those two attracting attention to him. Lionel slouched down and pretended to tie his shoelaces.

"Hi, Lionel," the blond boy said. "How's it going?"

Lionel wanted to literally kill him. Nick would notice three loser kids talking.

"I'm good," Lionel muttered.

Stephane was so clueless. No wonder he was Nick's favorite target.

"Do you know if Whellan is gonna make us read our stories tomorrow?" Jaime asked.

"No idea," Lionel said.

Whellan was their English teacher. He'd made them write a short story, and now he was forcing them to read it out loud — in front of everyone.

He glanced over. Nick had the ball and Bryan was running for a pass. The bell had to ring soon. He might get lucky.

"I'm nervous about reading my story," Jaime said. "I wish we didn't have to."

The ball nicked Bryan's fingertips and bounced to the fence next to Jaime.

"Bro, toss me the ball," Bryan said.

Jaime underhanded it to him.

"Another awesome grab from Bryan Butterfingers Klutz-Face," Nick taunted.

He and Mohamed had come over.

"Toss it to me," Nick said.

Bryan slipped it over.

Nick whipped the ball into Jaime's chest in one motion. It bounced back to him.

"Sorry, weren't you ready?" Nick laughed.

Jaime gasped, and then laughed uneasily, rubbing his chest. Stephane gripped his backpack straps.

"You wanna toss the ball around with us?" Nick said. He stepped closer until he was practically nose-to-nose with Stephane.

"Hey, Nick ... um ... not really. I ... School's about to start," Stephane managed.

Lionel slowed his breathing and looked down at the ground, pressing his back against the fence. He didn't dare move.

"Maybe another time?" Nick said.

Stephane nodded. "Sure. Maybe."

The three boys roared.

"Absolutely, bro. We gotta get out on the field and play some ball," Nick said.

He slapped Stephane on the shoulder. Stephane winced.

Nick looked over at Lionel. A big smile crossed his face.

"What about you? You gonna play ball with us?"

Lionel didn't react. He was looking into his backpack, as if he'd lost something inside.

"Yo, retard. Do you ever know what's going on?" Nick taunted.

Lionel pretended he still wasn't listening.

"Ha!" Nick screamed, karate-chopping his hand in front of Lionel's face.

Lionel slowly lifted his head. They'd throw some shade — and then go away.

"The kid is retarded. Told ya," Nick said.

He shoved Lionel against the fence.

"You a freakin' retard?" Nick yelled in his face.

Lionel barely moved a muscle. Inside, his head was ready to explode and he couldn't breathe.

Nick backed away and nodded at two girls talking by the doors. "C'mon guys. The ladies need some of our awesomeness ... at least mine, anyway."

He headed over, Bryan and Mohamed right behind.

"Those guys," Jaime muttered, rubbing his chest again.

"They just like showing off," Stephane said. "They're not serious."

"Nick is," Jaime said. "Yesterday I saw him slam a kid's head against a locker."

"Why?" Stephane said.

Jaime shrugged. "Because Nick's an idiot."

Lionel moved away from them. They were the idiots for drawing attention to themselves. He'd had it under control, and then they had to talk to him. Nick scared him to death. That voice. He had a way of yelling that brought Lionel back to when he was a little boy, and his dad would yell so loud Lionel would pee in his pants. Once, his dad noticed and called him "Pee-Pee Pants" for a few days.

Lionel broke out in a cold sweat over his entire body, and for a horrible second, he thought he'd pee himself right then.

Nick and his friends were laughing with Kiana and Rashmi. Nick and Mohamed played on the senior basketball team, and Bryan was on the track team with Kiana, so Lionel sort of got why the girls hung with them — sort of. They were jerks, but the girls didn't seem to care. These were popular boys, athletes, sure of themselves, funny, tough. They did what they wanted.

Lionel slouched down and made himself small.

Kiana was laughing. Nick rubbed her back. Lionel figured they were boyfriend and girlfriend. Nick was always talking to her in English and math.

The bell sounded.

Lionel stood up. He hated this place, but he was terrified of high school next year — things might be worse then. He could legally quit school when he turned sixteen, but that was three more brutal years.

Lionel steeled his nerve and pushed off from the fence. Nick and the girls were inside already, but there were others to watch out for. Lionel walked slowly, evenly, but not so slowly that anyone would notice. He kept his eyes down and his shoulders soft, but not slouching, his breath shallow and weak.

No one looked at him. He bet no one even knew he was there.

Stephane and Jaime were talking to each other.

"You should tell Principal Ryder. He can't throw footballs at people," Stephane said.

"Yeah, right," Jaime said. "Then he'll really kill me."

They pushed past Lionel and went inside. Lionel let people pass him, until he was almost the last to go in. He always made sure he wasn't too early to class. Best to get there when it was full and kids were talking. Then they'd ignore you as you took your seat.

His back was sweaty. Nick had once noticed a sweat stain on his shirt and called him "The Big Stink," which is why he always had some emergency deodorant in his backpack. He had math first period with Nick, and he was only a row over from him. After what just happened, he didn't want to take any chances. He might miss announcements, but he could probably get by without a late slip.

Lionel turned at the bottom of the stairs and went into the washroom. This was the least-used one in the school, and he'd spent his share of recesses here. He took the far stall. For a moment he was tempted to skip math altogether and stay, but Kiana was in his class too. She was worth the risk.

Once in a while, Kiana even said hi.

He felt incredibly tired all of a sudden. The entire day seemed so long, and it hadn't even started. He hoped it wouldn't rain — he wanted to eat lunch at the park, away from everyone.

When Lionel finally left the stall, he saw himself in the mirror over the sink.

He turned away in disgust — a big, fat nobody.

## Wednesday 9:00 a.m.

Lionel pulled his chair back noiselessly, slipped his backpack underneath the table, and sat.

"Hey, Kiana," Nick said. "You wasting your time at track practise after school, or you and Rashmi want to hang at Pearl's?"

"I've got to waste my time, sorry," Kiana said. "And after that I've got to get home and walk the dog."

Pearl's was a café around the corner. The cool kids in Lionel's grade had started to go there.

"The dog? Seriously? C'mon. It's on me," Nick said.

"I told my dad I'd do it," Kiana said, a little sharply.

"That's cool," Nick laughed. "I love dogs, too. Take pooch for a walk, for sure. Give her a kiss from me. Is it a she or a he?"

Kiana smiled and tossed her hair to the side. "She's a Britney."

Lionel kept his eyes firmly on his desk. He could picture Kiana with a dog named Britney.

"You ready for the Mr. Bore Show?" Nick said to Kiana.

Bore was Nick's name for their math teacher, Mr. Ghaboor. This was about as funny as Nick ever got.

Ghaboor came in before Kiana could answer.

"Good morning, class," he said.

Lionel closed his eyes and pushed on them with his palms. His headache had spread and was pulsating under his eyebrows. He might be able to get out of school today if it got worse. He had to get through this class. No way he'd ask to leave in the middle.

"We will continue our discussion of solving problems related to perimeter, area, surface area, and volume," Ghaboor said. "Please open your textbooks to page eighty-two."

The class erupted with the rustling of papers and books. Lionel turned to the page and held the book in his hands. Teachers thought a kid was totally into the subject if he held his textbook.

Lionel had even fallen asleep in class, and as long as he held on to his textbook, the teacher didn't bug him.

"Settle yourselves, please," Mr. Ghaboor said. "This is not the jungle. It is a classroom."

"Then why'd I bring my spear?" Nick said.

The room tittered.

Lionel chuckled. He didn't want Nick to think he was disrespecting him.

Ghaboor took a piece of chalk and began drawing a graph. A folded piece of paper landed on Lionel's desk. A chill ran down his spine. The girl next to him nodded at Kiana. Nick had taken to passing notes to Kiana the last few weeks. Lionel's desk was on the delivery route. Lionel tossed it on her desk and looked back at his book.

Kiana read the note and crumbled it in her fist.

"Who wants to map out the first area?" Ghaboor said.

Lionel ran his finger across the page of his book. He kept still.

"Yes, Mr. Marco," Ghaboor said.

This sounded like it could go on for a good five minutes. He pictured the video game he'd been playing. He was having trouble getting past one section. Skeletons and an ogre attacked a ranger. He had to polish off the skeletons, waste the ogre with his machine gun, and get into the forest before the vultures poured out of the valley and ripped the ranger apart. If that wasn't enough, his controller had started jamming. He needed a new one.

Another note landed on Lionel's desk. Ghaboor's head shot towards him. Lionel put his book on top of the note and began rifling through the pages, as if he was looking something up. Ghaboor looked away. Close call. Nick would kill him if Ghaboor saw the note.

"Thanks, Mr. Marco. Excellent. Let's move on to question two," Ghaboor said.

Another note arrived. Lionel wanted to scream. Nick and Kiana were driving him crazy. He waited until Ghaboor turned to the board and he tossed it over.

Kiana took a deep breath. She read the note, scribbled something quickly, folded it, and gave it back. Ghaboor was still facing the board. Lionel figured it was safer to toss it directly to Nick. He'd done it before. Lionel backhanded it with his left hand. It hit the side of Nick's desk and fell. Nick scooped it up.

"Mr. Nick, are you the janitor now?"

Nick laughed. "Sorry, Mr. Ghaboor, I dropped something."

"Indeed, you did. What was it?"

"Nothing … a piece of paper."

"What was the paper about?"

"Nothing … math."

"Math? On a little piece of paper. Most interesting. May I see it?"

Ghaboor began to walk between the desks. Lionel shot a look at Kiana. Her entire body was tense and she gripped the edge of the desk. Ghaboor held his hand out. Nick gave the note to him.

"Hmm. I have no objection to two students going to … Pearl's." Ghaboor looked at Kiana. The rest of the class was giggling. "But please make arrangements after my class, and please resist the temptation to pass notes. You're in grade eight, not kindergarten."

Ghaboor gave the note back to Kiana. She didn't touch it. She continued to stare straight ahead. Lionel felt bad for her. She was a top student, always getting As and answering questions. She never got in trouble, not like Nick.

"Okay, let us proceed to the second question. Who would like to answer?" Ghaboor looked around the class.

Lionel picked up his book again.

"Mr. Lionel, I haven't heard from you in a while," Ghaboor said.

Of course, they'd love that.

He shook his head.

"Would you at least try?"

Lionel didn't respond. He stopped all thoughts, like his body was separate from his mind, floating, watching from a distance. This would be over soon.

Ghaboor sighed. "Okay, anyone else? Yes, Ms. Tina."

The girl next to him tossed a note onto his desk. He put it under his book.

A foot hit him in the thigh. Nick glared at him and he nodded at Kiana. Ghaboor turned to the board to check Tina's work. Nick kicked him again.

"Do it," Nick hissed.

Lionel tossed the note onto Kiana's desk.

"Nice throw, blubber-butt," Nick whispered.

Lionel didn't bother with his book. Ghaboor wouldn't call him again. Teachers never double-call a kid who refuses to answer the first question. Lionel had figured out way back that they don't bother with dumb kids too often. He noticed Kiana open the note. This time she shoved it in her pocket. Lionel turned ever so slightly to his left. Nick was frowning.

Nick kicked him again.

"Thanks, jerk," Nick whispered. "Learn to throw."

Lionel shifted his legs so Nick couldn't reach him. He'd have to skip school tomorrow. He was too much on Nick's radar. In a day or two, if he played his cards right, Nick would forget about him and move on to someone else — or back to Stephane and Jaime. His back was sweaty again. This headache was officially out of control, too. He had to go home. He couldn't get through the day. He'd go to Mrs. Dempsey and hope Ryder wasn't there — Ryder would just give him an aspirin and tell him to get to class. He had to go home.

"Excellent, Tina," Ghaboor said. "Well done. Everyone turn to question seven. I want to go over surface area."

Lionel looked at the clock. Another twenty-five minutes — more like twenty-five hours — and this was only Wednesday. If he skipped tomorrow, it wouldn't be bad. Maybe he could even scam Friday off. It all depended on Ryder. He couldn't let her call his mom. Not his fault school sucked so much — or that his chest hurt all the time. He hated taking those anxiety pills, though. They made him tired and he felt spaced out. The pain was better. Probably something wrong with his head.

His mom had promised to order in pizza tonight from Big Ray's. He'd get the Italian sausage with a Vanilla Coke. Nick kicked him again.

Lionel swiveled completely to the right. Let him try to kick him now.

A note landed on his desk.

"It's for you," the girl said to him.

Lionel opened it slowly.

*You're a fat, sweaty lard-ass — and don't mess up the throw again.*

Lionel didn't react. He looked at his book. The words started to blur, like someone had thrown water on the page and had made the ink run. His head was going to explode. For a second he was tempted to ask Ghaboor to let him go to the office. Bad idea, though. The other kids would laugh and remember him. It would be worse when he got back. He needed to tough this out. A few more kicks and Nick would get tired of it and pick on someone else. As long as he didn't react, he'd be fine. That's why Stephane and Jaime always got targeted. They didn't know how to take it. A little pain, and it was done. Complain, and it would never end.

## Wednesday: 6:30 p.m.

"Destroy," the ogre screeched in a blood-curdling yell.

Two skeletons charged from behind a tree, swords brandished overhead. To the right, a flock of vultures, faces twisted in hate, swooped over the craggy rock overhang. The ranger raised his machine gun and fixed his viewer on the ogre. He hesitated only to enjoy the moment and then pulled the trigger — nothing.

Jammed.

The ogre raised his massive hammer and swung at the ranger's head. The ranger did a shoulder roll to get away. The skeletons pressed closer. The ranger pulled out his swords. Two-handed he'd have the advantage, and the vultures were far enough away he could escape on his horse into the forest. The first skeleton thrust his sword at the ranger's chest. He parried the blow easily and, with a sweeping slash of his right hand, severed its head off. The bones collapsed into a pile of dust and disappeared. The vultures' shrieks reminded him that time was pressing. The ogre was stomping across the field to get him.

The second skeleton sprang forward, sword extended overhead. The ranger almost laughed. Stupid move. He pressed the button. The ranger's sword remained by his side. The skeleton reared back and sliced into the ranger. His swords slipped from his hands and the ranger fell to his knees. The ogre jumped up high and brought a crushing blow to his head with his hammer. The ranger crumpled. His horse faded away. The ogre let loose a hideous victory cry and the skeleton danced a jig, his bones clinking and clanking to a macabre beat. The vultures plummeted downwards, a mass of repulsive blackness, and began to pick at the fallen ranger. In five seconds, he was gone. The screen went black and dark blobs of colored rain fell to the ground.

The ranger popped up again, machine gun in hand, the ogre

across the field, the two skeletons to his right behind the trees, and the vultures back in the valley.

Lionel squeezed his controller, rage momentarily overwhelming him. The stupid thing never worked anymore. He gripped the sides of the computer screen. He wanted to fling it across the living room. He could picture it, the screen in tiny pieces scattered on the floor. He imagined his mom and Brent staring at him, in shock. He'd shrug, real chill, as if he didn't care, and go to his bedroom and slam the door.

"Earth to Lionel. Can you understand English?"

"Brent, he can't hear with those headphones on."

"Charlene, nothing personal, but I think your kid is retarded," Brent said.

"You're so ... rude," Charlene said.

"Relax. He can't hear me," Brent chuckled.

Lionel punched the start button. He couldn't let Brent know he'd heard every word.

"Lionel, honey." His mom put a hand on his shoulder. "Lionel, do you feel like pizza for dinner?"

He pulled his headphones off.

"Does pizza sound good tonight?" she repeated.

"That garbage can will eat anything," Brent said. "Look at his gut. I bet he couldn't run ten feet without puking."

"Hush, Brent. You're being so mean tonight," Charlene said. She squeezed Lionel's shoulder. "You pick the pizza."

"I don't care," Lionel said.

He put his headphones back on. They'd leave him alone soon, and then he could game all weekend. Even his mom sometimes forgot about him. The trick was turning off your mind, breathing steady, dropping your head and shoulders a bit, and closing your eyes slightly. It worked every time, like he could actually disappear.

"We should be celebrating tonight," Charlene said as she walked back to the television.

"Don't jinx it," Brent said sharply.

She changed the channel. Lionel snuck a peek. Two guys and a girl were racing through a forest towards a flag. His mom loved this show — some challenge race.

"Let's watch the game," Brent said.

"I want to see the end of this," she said. Charlene offered Brent a bright smile. "How about we go to The Uptown later?"

"Don't feel like it," Brent growled.

"You're such a homebody. Take me out. It'll be fun. We'll have a drink."

"Ech. Not tonight."

"You go there all the time."

"Shut up about it," Brent snapped.

Lionel caught of glimpse of his mom's face. She looked tired — and sad. She flicked the channel and laughed.

"You're right. We'll go out tomorrow to celebrate the new job. I'm excited about it, that's all," she said. "Maybe we can go on a holiday this summer, like to New York or even somewhere sunny."

"You're spending the money already?" Brent said.

"I thought it might be fun for Lionel …"

Brent waved a hand in the air. "All he wants to do is sit in front of that computer and eat. He's a big Do-Nothing. What would he do on a beach anyway, other than look like a beached whale?" He chuckled to himself. "Hey, Lionel," he yelled. "Do you want to go to a beach or sit on your butt and game?"

Lionel felt weak all over and his chest hurt when he breathed in.

His thumb hovered over the controller button. The figures were fidgeting back and forth, waiting for him to give them life.

He put the controller on the table. He had to buy a new one. Maybe if Brent actually got that job his mom would have some extra money.

His butt was sore and he was hungry.

"Mom, what are you going to order?" Lionel said.

"Hush, Brent," she said. "I told you to choose, honey."

"You can," Lionel said.

"You guys are killing me. Pick the damn pizza already," Brent said. "You two would lose an IQ competition to a chair."

Lionel kept his eyes focused on the computer screen. A rush of dizziness swept over him, his head spinning faster and faster until his stomach began to sway and a bit of vomit came up his throat. It was happening again.

"I'll pick something," his mom laughed. "You are in a mood tonight, Brent. I think you're nervous about the job."

"I ain't nervous about nothing," Brent said. "My bro Fergus is gonna nail that job for me. You wait. And once I get it, it's easy street for yours truly."

"What do we feel about the Quattro Formaggio?" Charlene said.

"Fine. Doesn't matter," Lionel managed.

"If you don't want it ..."

"It's fine."

He ran to the bathroom.

Brent began laughing. "Your boy has the runs."

"Lionel, honey, are you not feeling well?" she called out.

Lionel closed the door and dropped to his knees, leaning his head over the toilet bowl. This had to stop, this getting dizzy and his stomach feeling queasy for no reason. Two days ago, in English, he thought he was going to hurl.

Smart move that would have been. *Puke Boy*. He'd wear that nickname forever.

For a second, he thought the vomit was coming.

Nothing.

"Honey, are you okay?" his mom asked. She knocked gently on the door.

Lionel sat down on the floor and leaned against the toilet. He couldn't answer. His throat felt full, like something was choking him.

"Honey. Answer me. I'm going to come in if you don't tell me you're okay."

She sounded worried.

"I'm okay."

"Okay, honey. I'm going to order the pizza."

He let his chin drop to his chest and he forced himself to breathe slowly. He prayed for his stomach to be okay before the pizza came.

## Thursday: 8:20 a.m.

Lionel took a few more cookies and finished his Coke. "I'm not feeling that well," he said.

"It's all that pizza you ate last night. I can't believe you and Brent," his mom said. "Like animals. Two party-size and all we have is a few pieces left. I thought we'd have enough for dinner. I'll see you after school. We'll probably all go out to celebrate Brent's new job. I'll send you a text, okay? He finds out after lunch."

Lionel shrugged and bit into a cookie. His head was still fuzzy. He hadn't slept much. The pizza had turned on him and he'd felt sick, his stomach tight like a drum.

"He's going to meet Fergus and get ready for his interview. Isn't it exciting? He'll be making twenty-five dollars an hour, plus overtime, and we can finally get that Visa bill paid off, and maybe buy a car, a used one, but it'll be nice to be able to drive places. I know he was being kinda nasty last night. He was just nervous. We'll go on a holiday this summer, somewhere sunny. Won't that be nice?"

Lionel finished the cookie. He moaned and put his hand on his stomach.

"Like I said, there's a bit of leftover pizza if you're hungry." She looked at her phone. "Shoot. I'm going to be late. Sheila's gonna nag at me, like it's such a big deal. If I'm so much as five minutes late she has a complete meltdown in front of everyone."

Lionel groaned again, but she wasn't buying it. He gave up and said goodbye. He'd have to time it perfectly so he wasn't standing in the yard before the bell rang. He had English first thing today. Nick was in his class, but then he was Nick-free for the rest of the day and he could chill.

He munched on another cookie. It was nice to be alone in the apartment. This used to be his favorite part of the day, after his mom left for work and before he had to leave for school. Until Brent moved in about three months ago and ruined it. Brent usually sat at the table and drank coffee, playing a game on his phone.

Lionel opened the fridge and took out another Coke. He tilted his head back and poured it into his mouth a couple of inches from his lips so he could feel the burn at the back of his throat. Slowly, rhythmically, he swallowed it down until the can was empty. With his thumb and index finger he squeezed the middle so the sides touched and then, using both hands, wiggled the top and bottom back and forth until the can split in two. He tossed the pieces in the garbage.

He went to his bedroom to grab his backpack. He swept aside some blue jeans with his foot, looked under a pile of towels, pushed a jumble of shirts and socks to the wall, threw a pair of underwear into his closet, and then saw a blue shoulder strap peeking out from under his bed. He pulled his backpack out and then noticed his underwear had hooked itself onto the doorknob — a miracle shot. He couldn't do that again in a thousand more throws.

Where'd he put his shoes?

He tried to remember what he did when he came back from school yesterday ... a Coke, then some nachos, then the computer ...

He found them up against the wall under the computer desk.

He shoved his feet in, locked the door behind him, and went to the elevator. An old woman, a cane in one hand and a large, white shopping bag slung over her shoulder, waited by the doors. Lionel pushed the button.

"I pushed it already. I may be old, but I'm not that senile," she laughed. She pointed to the elevator with her cane. "This elevator is the worst. Takes forever. I spoke to the superintendent about it, and of course he promised to look into it. That was two weeks ago, and it's still the same. Three days ago I wrote the company that manages the building. I'd tried calling, but all I got was an answering machine — and no return call, believe me. We pay rent and we deserve a working elevator. I'm too old to take the stairs."

Lionel stared at the floor. He was going to be late. Mrs. Dempsey would hassle him and give him a lecture and maybe even take him to Ryder. He considered going back home and gaming, except the last time he did that, the school called his mom at work and it turned into a huge deal — not worth the yelling. He stabbed the button a few more times.

He'd seen the old lady around the building. She'd moved in about a month ago.

The doors opened and they went in.

"I'm recycling," the old woman said, holding her bag up. "I complained to the superintendent that we didn't have a recycling bin outside and he finally got us one. Of course, he had to. It's the law."

Lionel stared at the buttons. Number one finally lit up and the doors opened.

"Take care," the old lady said. "My name's Donna, by the way. Have a good day at school."

He figured that meant he was supposed to leave first.

"So, what's your name?" she said, as he stepped out.

"Sorry … I'm … My name's Lionel."

"See you later, Lionel," she said.

"Goodbye."

He crossed the street and headed to the Market. It wasn't really a market. Years ago there used to be tons of stores in the area and the name just stuck. Now the Market was only a block long, with mostly run-down places. Manuel's Garage was open already, and he could see Manuel hunched under the hood of a car. Up ahead, across from The Uptown Bar, where Brent hung out, a man sat on a steel chair smoking a cigarette. He leaned forward and petted a dog who lay on the sidewalk in front of his feet. Lionel had seen the man a lot — he worked at Binny's Café. Sometimes the man said hi, which was awkward. Lionel crossed the street so he wouldn't have to talk to him.

At the end of the Market, Lionel turned the corner just in time to catch a glimpse of the bus pulling away. Perfect! Now he was definitely going to be late. The next bus wouldn't be by for at least fifteen minutes.

Should've stayed home.

## Thursday: 9:30 a.m.

Lionel walked into the office.

Mrs. Dempsey's jaw set. "Lionel, I don't understand why it's so hard for you to arrive on time. Do I need to buy you an alarm clock?"

"Sorry, Mrs. Dempsey."

She continued to look at him for a few seconds — and then her shoulders fell slowly and her eyes softened. "I have trouble getting ready in the morning, too. But I wish you'd make more of an effort. Principal Ryder is concerned about you."

Ryder had called him into her office two weeks ago and asked him whether he was happy at school, if things were okay at home, and if he needed any help. She told him her door was always open — which wasn't really true because it was closed right now.

He felt bad for Mrs. Dempsey. She had to deal with late slips, and it wasn't her fault he was always late. That was the bus driver's fault — and the elevator's.

"Sorry. Tomorrow I'll get up early," he said.

Mrs. Dempsey grunted and placed a strip of paper on the counter. "I should print off a pile of these with your name on it. It would save me time. You're finished grade eight in a few months, so I'll only need a few hundred, I reckon." She crossed her arms, and then lowered her head, shaking it slowly side-to-side. "Lionel, one of these days I'm going to make you laugh. It's become my mission in life. Don't worry — I've got better material. I'm just saving it up for the perfect moment."

He forced himself to smile. "That wasn't bad. I'm kinda tired. Had to run for the bus."

"Of course, the famous *missed bus*. That's one crazy bus you take. It disappears the second you get near."

Lionel headed down the hall and up the stairs to English.

The classroom door was closed. He should've waited until it was too late to go to class. Now he had to go or he'd get in trouble.

He reached for the door handle but it pulled away from his hand. He heard giggling.

"You've decided to join us, Lionel?"

Mr. Whellan had opened the door. Lionel glanced over Mr. Whellan's shoulder at the grinning students. His seat sat empty, two rows over, three back — next to Kiana. The first day of class he had pulled off a huge coup and got the seat beside her.

He gave Whellan the late slip and walked in, stone-faced, eyes down, all thoughts banished, disconnected from the unfriendly, staring faces.

"Thanks, Rashmi," Whellan said. "I liked your story. Nice character. She's smart, tough, and funny. That's the most important thing in a story, to create someone the reader cares about, and I cared about her. The plot is important too, and so is grammar and all the other elements of story-writing we've studied. But what I really want from you guys are characters that make me feel something. So what did you feel when you heard Rashmi's story?"

"Angry because her dad treated her so bad," Kiana said.

"Good. Excellent. What else?" Whellan said.

"Curious," Angelina said. "She had to decide what she would do next, and I had no idea what she would do — and that's the cool part of the story. You want to read more to find out."

Lionel tuned out. He liked being in a class with Kiana, Rashmi, and Angelina because they knew all the answers, so Whellan didn't bother picking other kids too often. He was a nice guy, really. He never embarrassed Lionel, at least not too often.

Last class, Kiana had read her story about a street kid begging for money to get something to eat. The kid ended up going to sleep hungry. Lionel loved listening to her voice, and he'd closed his eyes and let her words wash over him, forming pictures in his mind — intense, colorful. There wasn't much he didn't like about Kiana; she was so smart, and funny, and athletic, and popular. Even though she had all that going for her, she never treated people badly — never — at least he'd never seen it. Lionel had perfected the art of looking at someone without them knowing, and he'd snuck his share of looks at Kiana.

Jaime read his story next. It was about a boy who liked basketball. He was being bullied by the other guys on the team because he was the new kid at school and the best player.

"Pass the ball. Basketball's a team game."

"Why don't you go back to where you came from?"

Lionel tuned out again. He knew how Jaime's story would end. There would be a bully, the new kid would stand up to him, and the surprise ending might be the two kids became buddies because deep down they had something in common, like singing or something lame like that. Schools were obsessed with bullying, not that teachers or principals had a clue how to deal with it. He'd heard a hundred talks on it. The same stupid message: *Stand up to bullies because they're really cowards and insecure, which is why they bully in the first place, to feel good about themselves.*

In stories, the bully always backed down.

It was pure garbage — all of it. Bullies never got bullied. They did what they wanted. They had it made. His strategy was way better — don't let them notice you. Bullies don't bully what they don't see.

"I thought the imagery Jaime used, the storm and the dark skies, was a smart way to make us feel scared and worried."

"That's an interesting point, Stephane," Whellan said.

Lionel didn't get Stephane. He got bullied all the time because he was inviting it. He was always putting his hand up and answering questions in class, and he did the lighting for the school play, and he belonged to the photography club. He might as well wear a T-shirt that reads, "I'm a Geek — Please Beat Me Up." Nick and his crew made Stephane's life miserable. Lionel couldn't imagine how he got through each day, waking up knowing Nick was waiting, everyone was waiting to make him feel bad, and there was nothing he could do to stop it.

"Thanks, Stephane. I agree," Whellan said. "You did a nice job, Jaime. Good effort. I can only imagine how tough it was for Roger to deal with those bullies, and having Roger and the toughest bully in school become best friends was a clever twist. Now, I think we have time for one more. Who hasn't read theirs ..." His voice trailed off. He opened a folder on his desk and ran his finger down the page. "Lionel. What do you have for us?"

Lionel's face grew hot and his underarms got wet. He stared intensely at his desk. He couldn't believe Whellan was being such a jerk. He never did this to him.

Whellan drew in his breath and let it out slowly. "Maybe you need another couple of days? Would that help?"

Lionel dug the tip of his pencil into the palm of his right hand. The tip was broken so it didn't hurt that much. He nodded.

"Okay. We'll do that. Please make an effort, okay Lionel?"

He nodded again.

"Bryan, how about you give it a go? I think you're the last one," Whellan said.

Bryan's face flushed deeply. He gripped the pages of his story tightly and cleared his throat a few times. "The sky was black 'cause it was stormy. The rain fell hard on the ground and it was cold," he began.

Lionel ran his hand over the zipper of his backpack. He'd finished his story two weeks ago. Once he'd started, he couldn't stop: the words poured out of him and his fingers flew over the keyboard. It didn't even feel like homework.

Still five minutes left. Science next, which was okay because his teacher never called on him. Deadly boring, though. Then he had geography, then lunch, then math and art, and then he could go home. It would be cool to go to a restaurant tonight. Hopefully, they'd get burgers.

"You think you're so tough, but you're just a stupid bully," Bryan read. "I'm not afraid of you."

## Thursday: 3:35 p.m.

Lionel slipped around a small group of kids huddled in the stairwell. He stopped in his tracks. Nick was outside, leaning against the door. To get through he'd have to ask him to move. Better to walk the long way and go out the north door. But someone bumped into him.

"Excuse me, Lionel," Stephane said. "You stopped all of a sudden."

"I was … Sorry."

"No big deal. See you tomorrow."

Stephane slung his backpack over one shoulder and pushed gently against the door. Nick jerked away and peered in. Lionel turned to look in the other direction. Stephane pushed the door again.

"What's your problem, goof?" Nick said, stepping away. "Trying to break my back?"

"I was just trying to get out," Stephane said. "You were against the door and …"

"Bang the door into my head next time, why don't you?" Nick said.

"I didn't bang your head. I just tried to push it open a bit so you'd feel it."

Lionel slipped back up the stairs, his hands shaking and his chest pounding heavily. Sometimes he thought Stephane liked to be picked on. He had zero awareness. Lionel went out the north door and turned to the right. He'd have to cross the entire field to get to the gate at the top of the hill. This day was dragging on forever. There was no way he was coming tomorrow. He'd fake a stomach ache, or better yet, a fever. All he had to do was take a hot shower and then let his mom feel his forehead. It usually worked, especially if he waited until just before she had to leave.

He kicked at a clump of grass and watched the dirt spray about. He was tired. The stupid bus better not be late. He gave another clump a kick and headed up the hill.

His stomach tightened painfully.

Five kids were standing by the gate, kids he knew. If he turned around now he'd have to walk all the way to the other side of the school. He could hop the fence, but they'd love to see a fatso like him do that. He took a deep breath. He could pull this off. He lowered his eyes, slowed his breathing, slumped his shoulders, and walked in small, quiet steps. He put his hand on the gate to pull it open.

"I'm looking forward to your story," Kiana said to him.

Lionel felt a sharp pinch in his throat. He noticed Rashmi put her hand to her mouth. She was laughing and didn't want him to see. Lionel kept his head down and walked through the gate.

"See ya tomorrow," Rashmi said.

"C'mon, Lionel, at least say goodbye," Kiana said.

"Goodbye," he said, and kept going.

They weren't mean girls, just messing with him. He counted his steps — five, ten, fifteen. At twenty he relaxed his shoulders and loosened his fists. His "Goodbye" had been a bit pathetic, for sure. He slowed down, content to shuffle along, more irritated by hunger than what had happened. He turned the corner and continued until he caught a glimpse of his bus. A car had blocked the intersection to make a left, and his bus had to stop.

He was hungry and he wanted those leftover pizza slices; if he missed this bus he'd have to wait forever. He began to run. He figured he had a chance if the car took a little longer to make the turn. Each step hurt because the bottom corners of his backpack dug into his sides and his gut was bouncing around. Suddenly, the traffic cleared and the car turned. The bus jerked forward. Lionel tried to run faster, and he would have if there wasn't a choking sensation in his throat and a pain in his knees. Sweat broke out behind his neck and in the small of his back.

The bus had come to the stop and the passengers were boarding.

His head was pounding and his backpack felt like it weighed a ton. He needed to walk, just to catch his breath. The puff of the bus's hydraulics gushed out. He'd missed it! Damn it. Sweated up for nothing.

The bus let out another puff, and he heard the sound of the doors opening.

Someone was getting off at the last second. He could make it. He ran across the street and staggered to the closing door.

The bus pulled away.

Stupid, stupid, stupid bus, he thundered to himself. A few more seconds — the stupid, stupid, stupid bus couldn't wait for a few more seconds!

A surge of heat scorched his body, starting in his chest and spreading to his fingertips and all the way to his toes. The next stop was only three blocks, and traffic was brutal in this stretch. He ran back to the sidewalk and began to weave in and out of the pedestrians, more like fast walking than actual running. His left heel stung where the top of his shoe rubbed against his Achilles tendon, and his stomach jiggled so bad it was embarrassing — but he was gonna get on that bus. He was too hungry to wait.

He caught up fifty yards from the next stop, only to have his hopes dashed when a car turned and the bus sped on. It pulled in front of the stop — and then the light turned red. But he knew this intersection: the red light here took forever — it wasn't over yet. He couldn't run anymore with his stupid backpack slicing his back open, though. He took it off and carried it in his hand, half shuffling, half walking. It was all he could do to gasp some air every few steps.

He never caught a break. He was a Do-Nothing who couldn't even run fast enough to catch the slowest bus in the world. A picture of Kiana and Rashmi popped into his head, and he imagined them laughing hysterically at his running.

He staggered ten more yards and stopped, but the light was still red so he went another ten. Still red — a flicker of hope, so he kept going. Twenty yards away the light changed to green. The bus didn't move. He crossed the street, and in a final, desperate lunge reached the door and pounded on it with his fist.

The bus shot forward. He slapped its side. The driver stared straight ahead and drove off. Lionel dropped his backpack and rested his hands on his knees.

He began to cough violently, his belly shaking with each eruption. He tried to stand, but that made him cough harder and he had to lean back down. Two girls crossing the street gave him an odd look. Lionel knew them from school. They both began laughing. He turned away and the laughter died off.

## Thursday: 4:45 p.m.

Lionel stepped out of the elevator and shook his shoulders to chase off the chill. The air had cooled and he'd gotten all sweaty running for that bus. Of course, the next bus was late and he'd waited about thirty minutes. The pain in his chest had gotten way worse — naturally — just to make the day perfect. He was tempted to take one of his pills.

The smell of Indian food from the neighbors down the hall made his stomach growl. He opened the door to his apartment and walked in. The television was on. His mom pointed at him with a pizza crust.

"Hey, Lionel, how was school today?" She tossed the crust into the open pizza box on the table.

She'd eaten all the leftover pizza!

"I thought you were working extra today," he said.

He went to the fridge.

"I had a terrible headache and had to leave," she said. "Sheila was such a hard-ass about it, as usual, and wouldn't let me go. I swear my head was gonna explode and she thought it was funny. Likes to see me suffer, and I tell you, I almost wanted to die just to get back at her. Thank God Maria took my afternoon shift. I came home and crashed."

Lionel closed the fridge door. "You ate all the leftover pizza?"

"Sorry, hon. My sugars were crashing and I had to eat something. Brent called and said he can't go out for dinner tonight, which is totally fine because guess what?"

She looked so happy.

He remembered. "I guess he got the job?"

She clapped her hands and came over and hugged him. "He did. He's a pain in the butt most of the time, and he's cost me nothing but money the last few months, eating my food and not paying rent, but with his salary we can do a million things we couldn't before. He probably has to meet with Fergus. They'll have a lot to discuss, I imagine. But for now, you and I can order pizza again. How about the Sicilian?"

"I guess."

So much for burgers. The sound of the TV began to irritate him and he wasn't going to listen to Brent bragging about his awesome job. He cast a longing look at the empty pizza box and went to his room.

Typical Brent, the cheapskate. He got a new job and wouldn't even take them out to eat. Lionel hadn't eaten at a real sit-down restaurant in ages. Some kids went all the time. Nick, Bryan, and Mohamed went out to eat at Pearl's every Friday. Kiana and Rashmi sometimes went with them.

He needed to scream. The sound of the TV was like someone digging needles into his brain. He kicked at a pile of clothes on his floor. They hit the wall and slid down. He scooped up a towel next to his bed. It was still damp. He threw it at his closet, and it pulled off the underwear hanging from the door handle.

The towel caused the door to pop open. He noticed some boxes stacked inside. He'd forgotten about them. Weird how that surprised him. They'd been there practically since he'd moved in. Lionel pulled the closet door completely open and looked inside the top box — his Pokémon cards from when he was a kid. Unbelievable that he still had them. He looked in the next box. On top was a light blue booklet — a journal from school, grade three. He opened the first page.

*Hi, I am Lionel. I liv with my mum and dad in our aparttement. I play basseball a lot with my dad. He is big. I like Pokeman. I play with freinds Pokeman a lot. I love my mum.*

Lionel let the booklet slip out of his hands. In the bottom corner of the closet he spotted some red stitching — his dad's old baseball. There was too much junk in the way to pull it out, and he couldn't be bothered. Seeing the baseball had brought a lump to his throat. His dad sure loved baseball. They used to throw the ball around in the basketball court in the back of the apartment building for hours. Sometimes they'd go to the park to practice hitting. For a long time after his dad left, Lionel dreamed about them playing ball together. He wondered if his dad taught his new kids to play.

Lionel was useless at baseball. His dad had always been mad at him for not throwing straight or not playing hard enough. After he was gone, his mom never had enough money to get him into a league, or the time to take him to games, so he stopped. Maybe with Brent's new job?

Stupid idea. He sucked at sports.

He pressed his hands against his temples. This headache was ridiculous — almost as ridiculous as the television volume. His mom was flipping through channels. Pick something! He slammed the closet door closed and went back to the living room.

"Have you called Big Ray's?" he said.

He needed to get out of here.

"Give me a break, Lionel," his mom said. "I'm trying to relax for one second. I'm just watching this."

"If you call, I'll go pick it up and we won't have to pay for delivery."

"Delivery's a dollar."

He couldn't listen to that TV for one more second. "I feel like walking."

She groaned and rolled her eyes. "Fine, already. Give me the phone."

Lionel gave it to her. "Can I have some money?"

"Take some cash from my purse."

Lionel opened her purse. He took two twenty-dollar bills and left.

This headache could do him a big fat favour and go away, and so could the pain in his chest. He probably just needed to eat, but it was irritating. He punched the elevator button.

Waiting again — as usual.

## Thursday: 5:10 p.m.

Lionel crossed the street and went into the Market. Big Ray's wasn't far, two more blocks, and he hated being cold, so almost without thinking he began to jog slowly to keep warm. His shoe was still rubbing on his Achilles tendon, but the warmth beat the pain. It wasn't that bad, anyway, and in a weird way the hurt felt good. It took his mind off that TV, and Nick, and Brent, and his English story, and school — and everything.

Most of the stores in the Market were either closed or closing. Manuel's Garage was still open. There were two people inside. Binny's Café had its lights on too, but the sandwich board wasn't out front. He shuffled along, huffing and puffing and limping. The door to Binny's swung open.

"That's what I need to do," the man said to him. He held his big belly with both hands. He was the same guy who sat outside in the chair with his dog.

Lionel slowed down. Was he talking to him?

"How far you going tonight?" the man said.

Lionel had no idea what he was talking about.

"On your run," the man said. "How far you jogging tonight?"

The man thought he was jogging? Like a runner? Like he was actually going for a run?

That was kinda funny.

"Not too far — just up a ways — bit cold tonight."

"You're a better man than me, I'll grant you that." The man laughed and rubbed his belly again. "My daughter jogs. She tells me she loves to run when it's cold. Says once you get going you don't even notice."

Lionel ducked his head slightly. "I guess I'm the same."

They looked at each other.

"Have a good one," the man said.

"Thanks."

He had to run now. He started off. His foot was hurting, but he couldn't turn around to check if the man was watching or he'd look like a liar. He just needed to get to Big Ray's. He clenched his teeth, closed his fists, and grunted with each step.

As Lionel walked in, Big Ray looked up from the pizza he was slicing and smiled. Lionel smiled back. Big Ray was friendly and always joking.

"Li – o – nel," Big Ray sang out.

He always greeted him like that.

"Hi, Big Ray. What's up?"

"You better hustle home, bro. Your pizza will get cold," Big Ray said. "On your way back from school?"

"I came from my place to pick it up."

Big Ray opened his eyes wide. "I just sent it out. Your mom didn't tell me you were coming. You guys haven't picked up in ages — it's been all delivery. I was starting to take it personally."

Lionel's arms hung down at his sides.

"You okay, Lionel? You look a bit disoriented." Big Ray came out from behind the counter and put his hand on Lionel's shoulder. "You're all wet too, like sweaty."

Lionel stared at him wildly. "I'm fine. Bye."

He ran out the door and back down the street. Brent would polish off the pizza by the time he got back. That man could eat an extra-large by himself.

Everything began to hurt at once: his foot, his chest, his head, his knees. He pushed it all from his mind and kept going, on and on, pounding along the sidewalk, past the now-darkened Binny's Café, past Manuel's Garage. He kept going and going until he couldn't feel anything but the pain; it was just him, the pain, and the sound of his shoes smacking on the sidewalk. He pushed open the lobby doors and punched the elevator button. It was hard to breathe.

"Lionel? Are you all right?"

He hadn't noticed Donna off to the side.

"What happened? Are you hurt?" she said.

He managed to shake his head.

"Lean against the wall and catch your breath."

"I'm okay ... ran a bit ... I'm good."

Donna smiled. "You must be late for something unbelievably important. You look like you've run a marathon."

A fit of coughing came over him.

"Dear me, Lionel. Are you sick? Do you need to sit down?"

"I'll be okay." He swallowed a few more times and finally caught his breath. "I ran too far and lost my breath. Thanks." She seemed so concerned. He felt bad making her worry. "Thanks. Really. It's nice of you to ..." He couldn't think of what was so nice, other than not many people cared what happened to him, and it was weird that Donna would. She didn't even know him. He tapped the elevator button again and the doors opened.

Donna laughed. "A minor miracle, I'd say. You get going. I need to put these cans in the bin." She rattled a bag she was holding.

"I'll hold the elevator for you."

She patted his arm. "You're a good kid. Well-mannered. Not many kids are these days. You go."

He waved goodbye as the doors closed, and then leaned up against the wall and closed his eyes. Death by pizza. He could imagine the police trying to figure it out.

*Why did he have a heart attack?*

*Couldn't be because he ran anywhere. Look at him.*

It would be one of those unsolved mysteries.

He walked into the apartment.

"They delivered the pizza, Lionel. Sorry, I forgot to tell them you were coming," his mom said. "I texted you."

"Sorry ... didn't bring my phone."

"I called Brent. He said he'll be here in five minutes. We should at least wait for him, okay?"

He wanted to devour the pizza himself. Easy for her to say wait after scarfing the leftovers. He didn't answer. He went back to his room and sat on his bed. His legs had stiffened up and his foot was stinging. A blister had formed, a big puffy one. He lay down. His head had barely hit the pillow when he heard the front door open. He groaned and forced himself back up. No way he was letting Brent get to the pizza first.

## Thursday: 5:45 p.m.

Brent stood by the sink and pointed at the faucet. He was holding a duffel bag in his other hand and there was a suitcase by his feet.

"You've been sitting on your fat butt all this time and you didn't even hear this water dripping?"

Lionel thought about going back to his room and pretending he wasn't hungry. Brent had obviously been drinking. His face was red and puffy and he was speaking loudly.

"Turn the damn television off for once in your life," Brent said. "I mean, really. Is that all you do?"

"Brent, this is supposed to be —"

"Turn the damn thing off, woman," he roared.

She hit the button on the converter. The apartment went quiet except for the dripping of the tap.

Plop, plop, plop.

"You can't even turn a tap off, Charlene? Seriously? You're actually that useless?" Brent cast a furious look at her and twisted the knob. The dripping stopped.

"I can't believe I lived in this funeral parlour for three months — feels more like three years."

"I don't understand why you're being like this," Charlene

said. "You got the job. Everything's good. Think of all the things we can do."

He rolled his eyes, and a cruel smile spread across his face. "Sometimes I forget how dumb you are."

Lionel watched a tear fell down his mom's cheek. He was used to Brent's moods, but he'd never seen him like this.

"I don't know what point you're making, but let's not do this in front of Lionel ..."

"Lionel?" Brent snorted. He cast a fierce look his way. "He's more useless than you. He can do two things: game and eat. I've been hanging out with two members of the living dead — only you're not as interesting as zombies! At least they eat raw flesh, which is kinda cool. All you eat is pizza and burgers." Brent slapped the kitchen tap with his palm. "Is it too hard for you to get off your damn butt and turn off a dripping tap? Is it?" He sniffed the air. "This place stinks."

"Brent, please — Lionel," she whimpered. "This will make him anxious."

Spit had collected in the corners of Brent's mouth. "Don't worry about that sack of potatoes. He's more dead than you. He's barely alive. Ain't that right, Lionel? You alive or dead?"

Lionel had no words. His entire body was paralyzed. Brent was in a rage. His dad used to lose it too, and Lionel would end up getting a smack.

"The funniest thing is, you actually thought I'd stay here with you two life-sucking zombies once I got a job. Are you that dumb?" He slung the duffel bag over his shoulder and grabbed the suitcase handle. "Catch you later, losers." Brent stomped over to Lionel. "Pair of Do-Nothings is what you are. You hear me, Lionel? Can ... You ... Hear ... Me? A Do-Nothing."

Lionel struggled to breathe. He closed his eyes and braced himself for the blow.

Brent laughed and patted Lionel on the back.

When Lionel opened his eyes, Brent was at the open front door, leaning out.

"Fresh air. I love it," Brent said.

The door slammed shut. Lionel remained frozen in place, still terrified.

"Well ... come and have something to eat before it gets cold," Charlene said softly, and she turned the television back on.

Lionel came over to the couch and opened the pizza box.

## Friday: 8:20 a.m.

Lionel had barely managed to drag himself out of bed this morning. He'd taken a pill and he still felt groggy and disoriented. The guy from Binny's Café was sitting in his chair. His dog took a few licks of water from a dish, lowered his body to the ground, and dropped his head between his paws.

A few cars sped past. He figured he should cross the street or the café guy would say something. He hated having to talk under pressure, like when you run into someone and they make a joke and you have to make one back. He felt a swoosh in his chest, a sucker punch, the wind being forced from his body. He had to gasp for breath.

He looked over at the café. It was cowardly to cross the street just because someone might talk to him. The guy would say hi and that would be it. He might not say anything. He probably wouldn't even remember him.

He continued along.

"It's Marathon Boy," the man cried out. "How come you're walking?" His belly shook as he laughed, his eyes bright and full of life.

Lionel could've killed himself. Why didn't he cross?

"I'm going to school," Lionel said, running his fingers over the shoulder straps of his backpack.

"What school do you go to?"

"Winfields."

A woman came out. Lionel guessed she was about the same age as his mom, only more energetic and fit-looking.

"Gwen, meet Marathon Boy," the man said. "He goes to Winfields."

"Do you have a real name?" she said, flashing a mouthful of beautiful white teeth.

"Lionel."

"Nice to meet you, Lionel," Gwen said. "And don't mind Binny. He's always getting into other people's business. Can't help himself." She rubbed the back of Binny's neck. "Maybe you can go for a run with Lionel some time. He and Britney could use it."

So, this was the Binny of Binny's Café. Lionel looked at the dog. Britney. The name sounded familiar.

Binny scratched his dog's head. "Do you feel like going for a run today?"

Britney grunted and closed her eyes.

"Maybe tomorrow," Binny laughed. "We'll go extra far to make up for it."

Gwen rolled her eyes. "I've been after him for years to get in shape. He's awful, either behind the counter or plopped in this chair getting fat. Anyway … do you know our daughter Kiana? She's in grade eight."

That swoosh in his chest came back with a vengeance. Kiana's parents — and that was her dog! If Kiana found out, she'd tell her friends and they'd chirp him for weeks. He felt panicky, light-headed, and his knees got shaky.

"Of course he knows Kiana," Binny grinned, "the most beautiful, smart, funny, athletic girl in school. Reminds me of her mother."

Gwen blushed slightly, and slapped the back of Binny's head gently.

"I should get going. I gotta catch my bus for school," Lionel said. A girl stepped out of the door. She was dressed head-to-toe in black, both arms heavily tattooed. Her jet-black hair fell long to her shoulders, very straight, and her ears were covered in piercings. She also wore a small gold nose ring. Her bracelets jingled as her hands waved in the air.

"We're out of Ethiopian beans," she said. "Did you order any? It's been two days. What should I brew up?"

"Go with the Kenyan, Georgina," Binny said. "I'll order more today."

"You said you ordered it yesterday," Gwen said.

"I got busy — afternoon rush. I'll do it now. No worries," Binny said.

"It's always no worries," Gwen said. "For once I'd like worries — and for you to follow through."

Binny's eyes met Lionel's. The light had dimmed.

"So ... I go with the Kenyan this morning?" Georgina said.

"I guess so," Gwen said with an angry shake of her head.

"I gotta get going to school," Lionel said. "Goodbye." He began to walk away.

"See you later, Marathon Boy," Binny said. "Say goodbye, Britney."

Britney didn't stir.

No one was at the bus stop when he arrived — bad sign. It meant a bus had just come, which meant he'd have to wait, which meant he'd be late, which meant Mrs. Dempsey was going to be an unhappy camper this morning.

He sat on the bench. The bus wouldn't come for another fifteen minutes if he was lucky. But he was never lucky, like this morning when his mom told him she had a headache and was going to stay home, so he couldn't fake a fever. He pressed his back against the shelter.

The squeak of hydraulics roused him, followed by a mouthful of hot, gasoline-filled air. The bus had actually come early! He grabbed his backpack and got on. He sat down near the back. His stomach hurt and he was tired. Maybe he could get out of gym.

## Friday: 3:15 p.m.

The sounds of squeaking sneakers and basketballs being dribbled were mixed every now and then with Marcus's shouts of encouragement or quick pointers. Lionel watched from the side.

"The ball moves faster than you," Marcus said. "Pass, pass, pass. That's how you get easy baskets."

Marcus hadn't bought Lionel's stomach excuse. He had to do the stretching and sprints, but when the game started, he went off as a sub and never bothered trying to get on. His teammates ignored him, as always, happy to keep playing. He got picked for teams because the guys knew he wouldn't play. It didn't bother him because he got what he wanted in the end — to be left alone. Ten minutes to go and school was done — except for the shower. Everyone had to shower at the end of gym class — stupid rule.

Marcus came over to where Lionel's team was playing. Lionel lowered his head and stared at his feet.

"Excuse me, Mohamed. Did you forget something?" Marcus said.

The boys stopped playing. Mohamed looked up at the ceiling. "You're right. I'm supposed to bounce pass to Nick and then cut inside for the give-and-go, and instead I ..."

"Not a basketball forget," Marcus grinned. "More like a mom who's waiting outside for you ...?"

"Ech! Stupid!" Mohamed slapped the side of his head with the palm of his hand. "I'm totally spaced. Forgot my mom's picking me up early. Gotta get my braces tightened so I'll be more beautiful than I already am, as if that's possible."

"Tell them to yank the teeth out. That's the only thing that'll make you better looking," Nick said.

"Get some Botox while you're at it," Bryan said.

Mohamed laughed. "You can't improve on perfection, boys," he said.

"Don't forget to take a quick shower," Marcus called to him as he headed to the change room. "Your mom will thank you."

"Nothing will get the stink off him," Nick said, and the boys all laughed, including Marcus.

Mohamed pretended to smell his underarms and then held his nose and waved his hand in front of his face. Lionel wondered how Nick, Mohamed, and Bryan did it, always ready with an insult, never nervous in front of people, never worried about what others said. Of course, it was easy when everyone was afraid of you.

He should've thought of leaving early — then he could've showered alone.

Next time he'd tell Marcus he had a doctor's appointment.

"Yo, bro. Wake up."

Lionel scratched the back of his leg and sat up. His tailbone was hurting from slouching so long.

"You deaf? We need you for Mohamed."

Nick held his arm out towards the court. Lionel felt an intense heat on his face, like a thousand spotlights had suddenly turned on. Only a few minutes to go and Nick was bugging him to play — Nick of all people.

"I … can't. My stomach hurts," he mumbled. He wrapped his arms across his belly and brought his knees to his chest. He'd told Marcus he was feeling sick, so he probably should stick to his story.

"Guy's a pylon," Bryan whispered to Nick.

Nick grunted. "You can't even stand on the court and be useless?" He glared at Lionel.

Lionel wrapped his arms around his legs and rested his chin on his knees. Nick would go away if he didn't respond. He had the attention span of a flea.

Nick rolled his eyes. "Okay. You can't even be useless. Fine." He looked around and spotted Stephane. "What about you?" he barked.

Stephane got up and walked onto the floor. "Where do I play?" he said.

Lionel almost laughed out loud. Stephane was like a sheep wandering into a wolf pack.

"You cover Bryan," Nick said. "If you get the ball, pass it to me, okay?"

Bryan was laughing as Stephane came over.

"Wonder if I can get past him," Bryan said.

Bryan took the ball at half-court and began dribbling slowly. Stephane followed him in an awkward crouch, arms extended. Bryan cut to his left, but Stephane managed to stay with him and kept him from penetrating the key. Bryan bounce passed to a teammate on the right flank, who held the ball over his head, brought it waist high, faked a move wide right, and then threw it back in Bryan's direction ... but it didn't make it to him. Nick anticipated the play and managed to get a hand on the ball, knocking it away. Stephane picked it up.

"Dish it," Nick barked, cutting to the basket.

Stephane bounce-passed the ball and Nick scored with a reverse layup.

"The mailman delivers," Nick said, striking a body-builder pose.

Lionel leaned back against the wall and watched the second

hand of the clock tick along. The minutes felt like hours. The boys kept playing. Finally, the whistle blew.

"Into the showers," Marcus announced.

Nick took a shot. It hit the rim and bounced to Stephane.

"Shoot," Nick hollered.

Stephane tossed the ball at the basket. It hit the backboard, the rim, and then out. Bryan flung his fist in the air.

"We are the champions of the world!" Bryan declared.

Nick threw his head back and stamped his foot on the ground.

Bryan held his hand out to Stephane for a high-five. "Thanks for being you and missing a two-foot layup."

"Bro, you suck so bad," Nick said to Stephane. "Why do you even exist? How do you miss that?"

"I'm sorry," Stephane said. "I ... thought it would go in."

Bryan grinned at Nick. "I thought it wouldn't."

"Useless," Nick said to Stephane, and he turned and headed to the locker room, Bryan following along.

Lionel stayed back. Best to let the others get started on their showers, and then he could shower without anyone noticing him. He fiddled with his shoes for as long as he could. The last of the boys headed in. He got up slowly and ambled over, dragging his feet. The locker-room door opened.

"Hurry up and into the shower," Marcus said to him.

"I didn't play," Lionel said.

"Into that shower," Marcus ordered.

Lionel took off his shoes and socks, striking a disinterested air, all the while keeping a wary eye on the guys. He slipped his pants off and put a towel across his lap. Some of the kids were already getting dressed and the rest were waiting for an open shower. This was perfect. If he waited long enough, he might even be able to shower alone.

A few minutes later, the showers had mostly cleared out. Lionel took off his shirt, his heart pounding furiously. Perfect time to make his move. Nick and Bryan were busy talking to Marcus about the stupid school basketball team. Knees weak and stomach lurching, he walked to the showers.

Lionel reached under his towel and pulled his underwear off. Only two guys were inside. He pressed the button. The water hit him in the stomach and he had to twist the nozzle up. It actually felt good, but he wasn't about to laze around no matter how good it felt. He stuck his head under the shower for a second and let the water run down his back. That was enough. He grabbed his towel and put his underwear on.

The room was quiet when he sat back down, only five kids left. Nick and Bryan were gone, and better yet, so was Marcus. Lionel slipped his shirt on. It stuck to his back because he was still wet. He felt better with it on so no one could see his gross stomach. The wet made it tough to get his pants on, and he had to wiggle to slide them all the way up.

Suddenly, a weird weak feeling spread throughout his body — a weakness so strong he couldn't move. He had no energy — none — and his chest felt like it would cave in. He felt himself getting upset, like crying upset, out of the blue, out of nowhere. He tried his usual trick of emptying his mind, making the bad thoughts go away — making himself invisible. He'd done it a million times.

All he had to do was go.

But he couldn't. He tried taking a few deep breaths.

Then it happened. He'd blown his chance.

"You gonna play next class?" a kid across the room said to him.

The kid's name was Ian. He wasn't a big deal. Just a kid, but he was way higher on the pecking order, and Lionel could tell he was going to take advantage of this opportunity.

"I felt sick today," Lionel said. "I shouldn't have come to school."

"You were sick last gym class, weren't you?" Ian said.

"I should go to a doctor," Lionel said.

"Yeah, like a shrink," Ian said.

They all laughed. Lionel joined in.

"You're probably right," Lionel said.

The tears were coming. You can't disappear when you're crying.

"Play on my team next time," Ian said. "We need a permanent sub. I wanna play the whole game."

Lionel chuckled. "I'll try."

He got up and strolled to the bathroom by the showers. He had to get into a stall. One picture, one Facebook post, one Tweet, and his life was over.

He closed the stall door and listened intently. He heard the shuffling of feet, and then the locker room door opened. They were leaving.

Tears fell down Lionel's cheeks, misery washing over him in waves.

## Friday, 3:37 p.m.

Lionel ran from the school. His eyes were red. Anyone who saw him would know he'd been crying. He raced past a group of grade seven kids hanging by the gate. He kept his head down, eyes half open.

He charged up the street. His blister hurt. He didn't care.

The bus slowed to a stop about twenty yards away. He wasn't going to miss the bus today — no way. He was going home … now!

"Stop, you freakin' bus!" he yelled.

The bus drove off. He raced after it in a rage so deep and strong that the top of his head felt hot; a rage so complete, his entire body buzzed, and his muscles twitched; a rage so powerful that he didn't notice his blister, or his chest, or his knees. He slipped past a mother pushing a stroller. Two old men were hogging the sidewalk and he had to jump over a garbage bag to get by.

"Hold on!" he yelled at the bus.

Two women standing outside a variety store watched him in amazement. He didn't care. His rage took away his caring. A car bore down on him and the driver leaned on the horn. Lionel dashed across the street. The bus pulled up to the stop. Lionel lunged for the doors.

They opened.

They actually opened.

Lionel stared up.

"You comin' or what?" the driver said, eyes squinting into narrow slits.

Lionel gulped, struggling to breathe, and stepped up. The doors slid shut, almost clipping his backpack. The bus merged slowly into traffic.

Lionel dug his pass out.

"I think I know you by now," the driver chuckled. "You've been taking my bus since I got transferred to this route two weeks ago."

"Sorry," he said, still gasping for breath.

The driver looked over at Lionel. "What are you sorry about?"

"Oh, um … nothing."

"Then why'd you say sorry?"

The driver's teeth were small and even. Made him look a little like Binny's dog, Britney.

The driver let out a harsh, staccato laugh. "I'm only messin' with ya, bro" he said. "Good to hear a polite kid once in a while. In this job it's rare, trust me."

Lionel bowed his head and smiled, grateful he didn't have to answer.

"You go to Winfields, yeah?" the driver said.

Lionel nodded.

"What grade?"

"I'm in eight — grade eight."

"Like it?"

Lionel shrugged.

The driver chuckled, "I didn't much go for school, not my thing. Couldn't wait to get out. Didn't learn much in school, neither, except hanging with my bros and getting into trouble." He chuckled again. "I figure you're like me, yeah?"

"I guess."

"You'll get through it. We all do." He lowered his voice. "Then you find a job and sit back and enjoy life. That's why I like driving. No problems, other than idiot drivers — and my boss is impossible. Some of my buds get all wound up about him. I say, who cares? Let him be a jerk. He ain't getting under my skin. Besides, he ain't such a bad dude, just got promoted and the power changed him. He used to drive. I figure deep down he's still one of us."

The bus changed lanes and pulled up to the next stop. The driver screwed his eyes up again. "You need to move back from the doors to let the passengers in."

Lionel flushed. "Sorry."

"Heh …heh … heh," he chuckled. "You're always sorry 'bout somethin', yeah?"

Lionel shuffled to the rear doors. First time he talks to a driver and he gets dissed. He's probably the jerk, not his boss. He took his backpack off. His shirt was wet. The bus started off, and he leaned against a pole and stared out the window. He'd made it, though. He'd actually run all the way from school — and to the second bus stop — without stopping. For a second he almost burst out laughing; he even had to turn away and look out the window so people wouldn't see the stupid grin on his face.

He'd made it.

And he didn't have to be sorry about that.

## Friday: 6:45 p.m.

Lionel crunched the paper bag with his hand and tossed it on the floor.

"Is that for me to pick up?" his mom said. "I bring burgers for a treat and you make a mess? I don't think so."

Lionel took some fries.

"Um … Did you lose your hearing? I don't appreciate the disrespect. Don't throw your stuff on the floor." She began to cycle through the channels.

His stomach felt gross — hard and bloated. It had begun when he got home. For the first time in his life he didn't feel like gaming. He'd been so stoked about Brent not being here. It was Friday night and he could stay up as late as he wanted. Instead, he was wasting time watching his mom's stupid shows. Eating only made it worse — way worse.

"Lionel!"

He snatched the bag from the floor and slammed it on the table.

"And an apology, please," she said.

He wasn't going to say sorry. No chance. Sorry for what? The burger in his mouth tasted like chalk. He opened the bag and spit his burger into it.

"Thanks for that, too. I really needed to hear that sound. It's been a brutal couple of days, with Brent being such a jerk. And I have to work Saturday now, covering for Marcia who is going to the casino with Rory."

Lionel dug his fingernails into his hands. A spasm flitted across his stomach and up into his chest, like a flash of pain.

He tossed his burger into the bag.

"If you hate your job so much, why don't you get another one?" he said.

His mom grimaced, mouth open slightly. "You're a kid. You have no idea what it's like out there. Jobs like mine don't grow on trees. I'd never get the same money somewhere else, not after eight years, and I get benefits and three weeks' vacation. It's ... like ... impossible for me to leave."

"But all you do ..." He couldn't say it. She'd flip out.

His mom turned the volume down. "All I do is what, Lionel?" she said, glaring at him.

His dinner sat in his stomach like a bowling ball.

"All you do is complain and ... maybe I don't feel good all the time ... and it's hard to listen to you complain every second of the day."

"Excuse me? I complain every second?" She seemed staggered.

"Every other second, then — and you do. It's non-stop. And my chest's been hurting for a week, more like two or three, and ... You didn't ask me once how I was feeling. You're a broken record: 'I hate Marcia'; 'I hate work'; 'I hate Sheila'; 'I hate Brent'; 'I hate my life.'" He took a breath. "Well, I hate my life too, only I don't complain about it all the time."

"Lionel, honey. I didn't know you weren't feeling well."

"Now you do."

She closed her eyes briefly and came over to him. She began to stroke the back of his neck. "Poor Li-Li. You have to tell me when you're not feeling well, so I can take care of you."

He shrugged her hand off his neck and moved away. "I'm not a little boy. How about we stick with 'Lionel.'"

She pouted. "Not fair. I miss my little boy. When did you turn into a teenager overnight?" She reached out and he pulled away again. "I guess that's normal. You aren't a little boy, I get it," she said. "And maybe you're right … about me complaining. I think I just need a change in my life, that's all; but I don't know what to do. Maybe I'm bummed out about Brent."

"Why do you care about him? He sat around and stuffed his face and yelled at you all the time. He called us Do-Nothings."

She got quiet. "I guess I get … lonely sometimes, and end up making bad decisions, like thinking Brent and me had something together. I pretended Brent was someone he wasn't. All the signs were there. I just ignored them. I know I have to work on my confidence … Anyway, don't listen to Brent — as if we do nothing."

Lionel folded his arms. "What do we do?"

His question hung in the air.

"We … This is dumb. Lots of things. Don't be silly." She reached over and squeezed his shoulder. "We need to cheer up, you and me. I'm sorry for moping around. You're right about Brent, too. Don't know what I was thinking. He wasn't good for me — or you. He's forgotten. Over. Bye-bye." She paused. "Let's celebrate. Do you wanna go to the corner store for ice cream? You pick the flavour."

"I'm not that hungry."

She laughed. "Since when do you eat ice cream because you're hungry? The walk will do you good. We can watch a movie, whatever you want. It's Lionel night. I don't want my baby feeling sad. Grab some cash from my purse."

Lionel stared at the empty cups and the containers. His mom sat back in her chair and reached for the converter. "Go for it," she said. "Anything but that awful peanut butter stuff you bought last time. That was gross." Movie listings popped up on the television. "Do you want action, comedy, or a documentary? I know you love documentaries."

Lionel walked to the door.

"You choose," he said quietly. He slipped on his shoes, took a ten-dollar bill from her purse, and left, trudging to the elevator, barely picking up his feet, so his heels skidded on the carpet. The thrill of catching the bus was officially gone. He had no idea why. He pushed the button and the doors slid open.

"Please hold the elevator."

Donna toddled towards him carrying a large plastic shopping bag. Lionel stood in between the doors to keep them from closing. Donna stepped in. She wiped her brow and sighed.

"When did I become so slow?" She gave him a smile. "Where are you off to, Lionel?"

"Going to get some ice cream."

"That's nice — a little treat. Well, you deserve it. You're always going to and from school — and running about with friends, I bet. Can't touch the stuff myself, not any longer. My doctor told me I'm pre-diabetic. Can you believe I lost twenty pounds in twelve months? It's true," she beamed. "I go to the gym every day for my water aerobics, and then take a long walk, and I've cut out all the junk." She shook her bag. "Decided to do some recycling. I know I'm being silly. It's only Friday and the truck doesn't come again until Thursday. I don't have much, but it makes me feel better. I hate to forget."

"Do you need me to help?" Lionel said. The bag looked heavy.

"That's sweet, but I can manage."

"Are you sure? It's no big deal."

The door opened.

"To be honest, I think I'm doing this just to get out of my apartment. I don't know too many people in this city, and my son lives far away. I get lonely. Have a good evening, Lionel, and enjoy the ice cream for me."

"Goodnight, Donna."

It hadn't occurred to him that she was lonely. Donna was always happy. You never really know someone, not really, not even yourself. Like what's up with talking to that bus driver, or to Binny and Gwen, or right now offering to help with the recycling?

Or what about the crying after gym? If that happened again he'd get so pummeled it wouldn't be funny — Stephane times ten.

It was like he'd become two people: there was the old Lionel who knew how to keep out of people's way, who could be invisible when he needed to, who didn't have problems with people because people didn't have problems with him; and then there was this other guy who cried and ran and talked to everyone who'd listen.

And the weirdest part of it?

He wasn't sure who he liked better.

## Friday: 7:12 p.m.

He was so busy thinking about the two Lionels that he didn't see Binny and Britney until it was too late to cross the street.

Binny waved. Lionel had to wave back.

"Marathon Boy is on the move. You ever stay put in one spot?"

Lionel grinned awkwardly.

"Out for your run?" Binny said.

He shook his head. "I usually run in the mornings."

"I'm opening the café tomorrow morning, me and Brit; don't forget to come by and say hi," Binny said. "I'll juice you up. Gotta keep hydrated when you run, right?"

"I guess so. But you don't have to … I bring a water bottle."

No harm in pretending.

Binny laughed. "Business ain't that bad that I can't spare some juice for a friend. Besides, you're gonna be in the Olympics one day and I'll be able to say I helped with your training."

"I think Britney will make the Olympics before me," Lionel said.

Binny let out a roar. "I'd pay to see Britney in rhythmic gymnastics — or the balance beam."

"She might be more of a shot putter," Lionel said.

"Ain't that the truth," Binny said. He gave Britney a head rub. Britney responded with a high-pitched whine and lay her snout between her paws.

The door opened.

Lionel's heart nearly pounded out of his chest.

"Lionel? What are you …? Do you live around here?" Kiana asked.

"I figured you knew each other," Binny said. "Lionel's a runner too. He runs in the mornings."

Lionel immediately stared at the ground. This was bad, a disaster. She'd tell Nick.

"I didn't know you ran," Kiana said. "You should come out for the track team. We need guys."

He knew she was just joking around. "Maybe," he laughed.

"Are you going to take Britney for a walk?" Binny said to Kiana.

"I can't. I'm meeting Rashmi," Kiana said.

Gwen came out. "It's after seven, Kia. Not too late, please."

"Mom, it's Friday night. I have all day tomorrow for homework," Kiana said.

Lionel needed to leave — fast.

"Who's going to take Britney for a walk?" Gwen said. She gave Binny a hard look.

He groaned. "Don't make me walk. I'm so good at sitting."

"I should get going," Lionel said.

"Me too," Kiana said.

"Home by ten," Gwen said.

"Mom, c'mon. Eleven thirty," Kiana said.

"Binny?" Gwen said.

"Oh, let her go. Life is short," Binny said.

"You're the best," Kiana giggled. She kissed her dad's cheek. "Bye Mom. Bye Lionel."

Binny let out a booming laugh, and Kiana set off down the street.

"Take care, Lionel," Gwen said, and she went inside.

Binny began to pat Britney. "You know, Lionel, I think I have a win-win kinda idea. Do you have a part-time job, by any chance?"

"Not really."

"If you have any extra time, like after your runs or after school, or any time really, maybe you could walk Britney for me and I'll pay you for it. That way I get Gwen off my back, Britney gets some exercise, and you make some cash for the new phone I bet you want."

"I could walk her sometimes — maybe after my runs," Lionel said. "I usually have a bit of time."

He obviously wasn't going to. He felt bad about lying, but he needed to get away.

"Awesome," Binny exclaimed. He clapped his hands and then rubbed Britney on the back. "Hear that, girl? You're gonna go for walks with your new friend, Lionel." He looked over. "When do you think you can start?"

"Tomorrow morning … um … after my run?"

Binny held Britney's snout in his hands and he leaned forward. "You're going for a nice walk tomorrow. That sounds fun. Right?" Britney licked his nose. "I think that means yes," Binny laughed.

Lionel said goodbye and continued up the street to the corner store. Run tomorrow? Have a heart attack, more likely.

He went to the corner store and peered into the freezer. He grabbed a carton of ice cream, paid, and left the store. He crossed the street and, head down, walked as fast as he could past the café.

As he walked up the sidewalk to his building he heard shouting. A man with a black leather jacket and silver studs gestured to him with a beer bottle.

"Hey, you need anything, bro?" the man said.

His buddies laughed. They belonged to a group of guys that called themselves the "Hombres." His mom was always freaking out about them. She called them a gang — maybe they were. Lionel was just as scared of them as she was, and figured them for dealers. They hung out most nights behind the building on the old basketball court. Cars and people came and went.

Lionel made a beeline for the door. He knew better than to talk to them. Fortunately, the elevator came quickly. He walked into the apartment and pulled the ice cream from the bag. His mom's shoulders drooped and her eyelids flickered.

He looked at the label — peanut butter.

"Lionel?"

He stared at the carton. "It's all they had. Sorry."

"Well, no matter," she sighed. "Even peanut butter ice cream is better than no ice cream at all, right? Can you get me some? Thanks." She leaned back and changed the channel.

Lionel put four scoops in a bowl, put the container in the freezer, and gave his mom the bowl.

"I'm full from dinner," he said. "I ... don't think I'll have any. I'm gonna lie down."

"Do you still feel bad, dear? I picked out a documentary for you," she said.

"I'm fine, Mom. Just tired. It was a wicked day at school."

"Are you sure you're not sick? It's only eight o'clock."

"I probably just need a good sleep. That's all. Don't worry."

"I have to work tomorrow, so don't sleep the day away. I swear you'd sleep twenty-four hours straight if I let you."

That was true. He loved staying in bed on the weekends. The time passed faster.

Lionel went to his room and closed the door. He looked down. He was standing on a pair of jeans. Towels and T-shirts were piled up in the middle of the floor. Clothes were tossed everywhere. His closet was so jammed it couldn't close. He picked up the jeans and folded them. There was nowhere to put them. He dropped them to the floor and sat on his bed. He pulled a towel from under his bed and threw it on top of his jeans. He pulled another shirt and some socks out and tossed them on the towel.

"Clothes hill," he declared.

He got down on his knees and dragged more clothes from under his bed, and then from around his room, and added them to the pile. Before long it was three feet tall.

"Now what?" he asked.

It was the most senseless thing he'd ever done — a pile of clothes and towels and sheets.

Lionel began to fold. It took a while, but he finally finished. He went over to his dresser and opened the first drawer. It was packed with candy wrappers, string, a broken flashlight, some gum, and half a donut. It was disgusting. He went to the kitchen.

"This documentary is interesting," his mom said. "It's about kid soldiers in Africa."

"I've seen it," he said. He took a few garbage bags and started back to his room.

"What are you doing?"

"Nothing. Going to bed."

He didn't know what he was doing. He dumped the junk in the first drawer into a garbage bag. Then it was on to the second drawer — full of clothes he hadn't worn since he was in primary school. He spotted a small baseball cap. He slipped it on his head and kept sorting. He put the old clothes into the bag. The third drawer had clothes he still wore, and some toys and cards and folders and old school projects. He got rid of everything but the clothes. He then folded them and added them to the others, organizing by type.

Once he'd finished with the dresser he kept folding, refolding, and piling. He organized and re-organized his room, working at a feverish pace, without thinking, rushing from corner to closet to under his bed, frenzied, even desperate — boxes, clothes, hangers, bits of food, and broken toys all got put in their place. He had to get three more garbage bags to handle all the junk.

His mom had gone to bed long ago, but he didn't stop. He got a broom, a mop and pail, and some cleanser, and dusted and scrubbed the floors, and the walls, and the inside of the closet, even under his bed.

He looked at his desk clock: one thirty. He was drained. His eyes were stinging. He was covered in sweat.

And his room was spotless.

On the desk he'd kept one box — his baseball and hockey cards, which he figured would be worth something one day, and his dad's baseball.

He took the garbage bags to the hallway and threw them down the chute. The crashing sound was oddly satisfying. He went back to his bedroom and sat on his bed. He took off the little hat. Stupid that he kept it. It was his baseball cap from the last year he'd played, before his dad took off. It had a P on the front — for Penguins. Before the games, their coach would tell them to waddle onto the field. His dad said that was stupid, so Lionel didn't do it. The other kids and their parents thought it was hilarious.

His legs shook slightly and his knees hurt, but his chest didn't ache, and his stomach and head felt good.

He didn't know why — he just felt better.

### Saturday: 9:30 a.m.

The light changed. He groaned and began to jog across the street, struggling for breath, each step torture. The bandage on his blister was useless, and his heel hurt too. This run had become an obsession for him last night after he'd finished cleaning. He lay awake in bed for a long time, thinking about it, and going over potential routes.

The reality of running was a lot different, however.

Marathon Boy? More like Joke Boy.

The Market was up ahead. He had to look like a runner for at least a block. He straightened up and threw his shoulders back. All he needed to do was keep up a nice, even pace. He pushed the pain aside and continued to the café.

No Binny.

He looked through the window. Georgina was behind the counter, serving a customer. Lionel jogged on the spot. Should he wait?

His blister started to hurt. He was sweating like a pig at eight in the morning to show off to a guy he barely knew. This was lame, even for him — the old Lionel, the Do-Nothing Lionel, the only Lionel there was. A bitter taste rose up from his throat and settled in his mouth.

"You're up early," Binny said, stepping out of the café. "Done your run already?" He stuck a long pole into the corner of the awning. He began spinning the pole, and the awning extended slowly out over the sidewalk. "Looks like you worked up a pretty good sweat. How far did you go?" He spun the pole energetically.

Binny's question startled him. "Not too far," he managed, almost laughing out loud. "I hurt my foot. I didn't bandage my blister very well and the bandage fell off and … Dumb of me."

The door opened and Gwen stuck her head out. "Where'd you put the Ethiopian coffee? Georgina says the container under the counter is still empty and I didn't see one in storage."

"Come say hi to Lionel," Binny said. He'd leaned the pole against the wall.

Gwen's braided hair was tied up with a bright yellow scarf. Kiana wore her hair like that sometimes. "Are you here to take Britney for her walk? At least someone isn't lazy."

Binny laughed good-naturedly. "Our man has been hurt. Wounded hoof. You wanna put it off today?"

"I'm okay," Lionel said quickly. "It's fine if I don't run."

The least he could do was walk the dog.

"What happened?" Gwen said.

Lionel pivoted his foot to show her.

Gwen let out a gasp and put a hand to her mouth. "My goodness. It's bleeding. That's terrible. Did you do that this morning?"

"I did it a few days ago, running for a bus. It's not too bad."

"You went for a run with a blister like that? You're certainly a tough young man, but not too smart. Runners have to take care of their feet." She took a closer look. "Are those your regular joggers?" she asked abruptly.

He nodded.

"I'll tell you what," she said. "I'm a runner too, like my daughter; I can't let you run in those. What do you think, Binny?"

"Absolutely not."

Gwen opened the door. "Hey, Kia, come here."

Lionel tried to keep calm.

Kiana wore black yoga pants and a yellow track top with the zipper undone.

"Come with us to Rajeev's. Lionel needs a pair of proper jogging shoes," Gwen said.

"You're jogging with Britney?" Kiana said.

"I … I'm not … We're walking, maybe," Lionel stammered.

"Look at those ridiculous shoes he's running in," Gwen said. "We can't have that. He has the absolute worst blister."

Kiana furrowed her brow. "You run in those? No wonder you got a blister."

"I was stupid — ran for a bus."

Gwen took Lionel by the arm. "Order the Ethiopian beans already," she said to Binny, and she led Lionel up the street.

"Never a moment's peace," Binny sighed.

"You'd have a moment's peace if you worked harder," she snapped. She pulled on Lionel's arm again. "This way. We need to talk to my friend Rajeev."

They headed towards Big Ray's. He wondered where they were going. He'd never heard of Rajeev.

"Kia tells me you're in her math and English class," Gwen said.

He felt himself blush.

"Have you read your story out?" she pressed.

His chest got tight.

"Kiana's story was great," he said to avoid the question. "Best in the class."

"Hardly," Kiana said.

"We should cross the street," Gwen said.

She was taking him to Adler Shoes. Who was Rajeev?

"You're certainly a quiet one," Gwen said, smiling at him. "Wouldn't last too long in our family. We never shut up."

She was kinda pretty when she laughed. Not as pretty as

Kiana, but he could tell where Kiana got her looks, especially her hair and her smile, and her beautiful teeth and skin.

He wished he could laugh like that — just laugh whenever he wanted. Kiana was always laughing.

They walked into the store.

"Rajeev, how are we this grand morning?" Gwen said in a loud voice.

A man behind the cash register turned around. "I am very well, thanks. How are my two beautiful ladies?"

"Always such a gentleman," Gwen said.

He came out from behind the counter and kissed her on both cheeks, and then Kiana. He was short, a little stocky, with a pot belly, and he had thick, black hair that swooped to the side. His eyebrows were bushy, almost too big for his face. A young boy came out from the back, very skinny, with black hair and a narrow face, and he wore a dark hoodie and bright white basketball shoes.

"This is Lionel," Gwen said. "He needs some joggers, good ones. I'm buying, so go easy on the price. Lionel's gonna walk Britney for us. We met him when he was running — runs past us in the mornings."

"You must run before I open because I haven't seen you jogging before," Rajeev said. "What size are you?"

"I'm ... a ... um ... not totally sure — a ten?"

Rajeev chuckled. "I'm guessing you're an eleven-and-a-half or a twelve," he said. "Big feet. You'll be tall someday." He pointed to a bench. "Deepak, can you get me the measure?"

Lionel sat. Gwen took a magazine from a stand and began reading. Deepak gave Rajeev the measure.

"How is the track team shaping up?" Deepak said.

"I think maybe we're going to suck," Kiana said.

"I was speaking about the girls' fifteen hundred," Deepak said.

Kiana elbowed Deepak in the ribs. "Weakest part of the team."

Deepak elbowed her back. "Why doesn't the girl who runs the fifteen hundred train harder? Is she lazy?"

"She's addicted to chocolate. It's a sad story," Kiana said.

Deepak spoke to Kiana like she was just another kid. Lionel could barely keep from stuttering when she was around.

"Would you be so kind as to remove your shoes?" Rajeev asked Lionel.

He'd been so busy listening to their conversation he'd forgotten why he was there. Lionel took them off.

Rajeev's eyes grew wide. "Your foot is bleeding! Dear me. May I take a look?" He pulled the sock off and let out a whistle.

Lionel was mortified. His toenails were long and gross. Kiana would be disgusted.

"That's a nasty blister, my friend," Rajeev said. "You cannot possibly run in this condition. We must tend to your injury first."

"I'm okay …"

"Deepak, can you get the first aid kit, please," Rajeev said.

Deepak brought him a white box. Rajeev took out some bandages, a needle, a bottle, tape, and scissors.

"I'm going to have to pop your blister to get the fluid out," Rajeev said.

"Gross," Kiana said.

"Awesome," Deepak said. "Make it explode."

"Deepak, please," Rajeev admonished. "It won't hurt at all." He lit a match and put the end of the needle in the flame. "Hold still for a moment."

He stuck the needle in. It didn't hurt.

"Oh, gross. It's spraying," Kiana squealed.

"Yum, blister juice," Deepak laughed.

Lionel wanted to crawl into a hole and die. It was gross. He was gross.

"This might sting a bit," Rajeev said. He dabbed the blister with antiseptic.

It did hurt, but Lionel didn't dare show it, not in front of Kiana.

"He's a road warrior," Deepak said. "Totally eating the pain."

Rajeev put a bandage on and taped it up.

"I declare the operation a success," Rajeev said.

Deepak and Kiana clapped.

"Now for the shoes," he continued. "Please put your foot in the measure, so I can …" He whistled again. "Exactly what I thought. Eleven-and-a-half. Hmm. Let me ask you, Lionel. Have you a color preference?"

Lionel didn't want to be rude. "It doesn't matter. Up to you."

"Because I have a shoe left in your size. It's somewhat unique, perhaps even peculiar, but it's a fantastic shoe, the best. Unfortunately, my customers did not warm up to the color. It is, what they say, fashion forward. The shoe salesman gave me a deal — and I suspect he did it because of the color. In any event, I bought them and have had no luck selling them. But if you're not too fussy — and it sounds like you're a serious runner — they might be just the thing for you, just the thing." He gave Lionel's knee a slap and stood up. "Give me a moment and I will get them for you." He disappeared into the back room

"How's it going, Lionel?" Gwen said, lowering her magazine.

"Good. He's bringing some shoes for me."

"What color are we talking about?" Kiana asked Deepak.

Deepak flicked his eyebrows. "Wait for it."

Lionel didn't like the sound of that. He pressed his hands together and stuffed them between his knees, rocking slightly back and forth. He was feeling bad about lying. This whole thing was wrong.

"You don't have to buy me the shoes," Lionel said to Gwen. "I don't mind walking Britney. I like dogs. My shoes are fine.

The blister is because I ran for a bus and … I did a lousy job on my bandage."

Gwen's eyes shone. "I want to buy them," she said, putting the magazine down. "Rajeev comes to the café about five times a day and talks our ears off; this is payback. And you can't run in those. Feet are your wheels. I know."

"Mom got a track scholarship at university," Kiana said. "She ran the one hundred and ten hurdles. Almost made the Olympic team, too."

"What happened … with the track?" Deepak said. "I didn't know you almost made the Olympics."

Gwen smiled shyly. "Got invited to the national trials one year — then life got in the way. I married, had a baby," she nodded at Kiana, "and, well, I had to stop training. Anyway, Kiana seems to have inherited the running gene from me, although she's more into long distance. Last year she made it to the city finals. Came second." She looked at Lionel. "You two should train together. It's hard to motivate yourself when you run alone. I try to get out with her, but it's hard to find the time."

Lionel's heart felt like it would drop out of his chest.

"I'm too slow," he mumbled.

"It's no big deal," Kiana said quickly.

Gwen opened her magazine. "No problem. Just an idea."

"Sorry for the delay," Rajeev said. He hurried over carrying a box. "This was buried under some other boxes. I must organize the stockroom better." Rajeev looked around. He coughed into his hand, sat on a stool, and opened the box.

This time Lionel's heart didn't just drop, it plummeted. An uglier pair of shoes he'd never seen. The color was only half the problem, which was saying a lot since they were bright green, almost neon, and the soles were olive yellow with a thin green line dividing them into two sections. But the most hideous part was a cheetah sketched in outline on the outsides, in full flight, paws extended forward and back, with a pained expression that made it look like it needed to go to the bathroom. The shoes' tongues had a bull's-eye symbol in the middle — green, yellow, and red. The laces were so green it was hard to look at them.

Rajeev began explaining why the shoes were so fantastic, something about the use of ultra-light materials, the soles being filled with air pockets, and the tension and compression of the rubber calibrated to maximize thrust. Lionel wasn't listening. The ugliness drowned Rajeev out. Kiana was trying not to laugh.

"These shoes cost about five hundred dollars in a real sporting-goods store," Deepak said, holding them up for Lionel. "A professional might use them, an Olympian even. Serious runners would kill for them. Sure, the color is a bit … intense." He handed Lionel the shoe. "Once you put them on you'll never take them off. They're that good. I wish I had a pair. We just don't have anything in my size."

"I believe we might …"

"I checked," Deepak said, cutting his father off.

Lionel slipped the shoe on. Fit like a glove, a second skin. He put on the second and tied them up. He stood — like standing on air.

"How do they feel?" Kiana said.

"Nice."

"You have to run around," Deepak said. "You can't get the feel of a running shoe without running."

"Absolutely," Rajeev said. "If you like them, they're yours. I insist you have them. A friend of Gwen and Kiana's is a friend of mine."

"You're so sweet," Gwen said.

"I guarantee this will be the last blister of your life as long as you wear these shoes," Deepak said.

Lionel was too frazzled to answer. He went to the door in a daze. One stupid comment to Binny and he was about to run down the street in mad green runners. He'd be the school clown if any kids saw him. Nick would come up with a name, for sure.

The Big Greener?

The Green Snot?

The Green Blob?

He started off.

They felt kinda good.

## Saturday: 10:15 a.m.

Lionel tugged on the leash. Britney seemed more interested in sniffing than walking. They'd only gone two blocks in about half an hour.

"Okay, girl. Enough sniffing," he said. "We're going to walk a bit faster." It was the least he could do after Gwen got him the shoes. He also wanted to do it for Kiana, to show her that he wasn't completely useless. He pulled on the leash and set off. Britney put her front paws out and began to slide, but once Lionel showed he meant business she ambled along for a couple of more blocks.

"It's nice to get outside, isn't it?" Lionel said to her. "Why don't we try running — real slow? Dogs should run. You're made for it."

They began, more like a quick walk, and before long Britney was panting like a steam engine, her tongue hanging out to the side. Lionel worried she would make herself sick, but she seemed to be enjoying it — and he liked the shoes. With the old ones he'd felt a jolt up his back with each stride. These absorbed the shock.

"A couple more blocks? Then we'll head back."

Britney let out a yelp, first limping to a stop, and then crumpling to the sidewalk.

"What's wrong, girl? Tired?"

She whimpered and began licking her front right paw. Lionel felt sick to his stomach. She was hurt; she'd probably stepped on something sharp. He tried to take a look, but the second he touched her paw she let out such a howl he let go. Could it be a broken bone? Had he gone too fast? Stupid. Britney hadn't run in ages and here he was pulling her along the street like a maniac. Britney began whining louder and louder. Lionel swept her up and she dug her snout in the crook of his arm.

He began to run back to the café.

This never would've happened if he'd just stayed home.

His arms shook as he raced past Big Ray's. Britney had quieted down and wasn't moving at all, as if she was growing weaker. He didn't see any blood. What was happening? Maybe she was bleeding internally. He barged into the café. Binny was behind the counter by the espresso machine. Gwen was talking to a customer. Deepak and Kiana were sitting at a table with another kid. Lionel recognized him from Manuel's Garage. He worked there a lot. Must be Manuel's kid.

"She sure is getting the royal treatment," Binny chuckled.

Sweat dripped into Lionel's eyes. He wiped his forehead. "It's Britney. I'm sorry. I got her to run, made her run, and now … something's wrong with her foot."

Britney began squirming. Lionel tried to hold her, but she dug her paws into his ribs and pushed off. Lionel gasped. Britney landed on her front paws. He reached for her.

"Don't put any weight on it," Lionel said, frantically.

Britney trotted over to Kiana. She held her snout and rubbed her head.

Binny handed a customer a cup of coffee. "How far did she make you carry her?" he grinned.

Lionel stared back.

Everyone burst out laughing.

"She totally punked you," Kiana said. "We should've warned you."

"She was faking it?" Lionel said.

"She started doing that when she was a puppy," Kiana said. "She cut her foot and my dad carried her home. Since then whenever she's had enough walking, which is all the time, she flakes out and waits for someone to pick her up."

"I was hoping she wouldn't do it because she doesn't know you," Binny said. "She's smarter than I give her credit for."

Lionel was too relieved to be mad. "She's a good actor," he said.

"You're just a big fat liar, aren't you?" Kiana said to Britney.

Lionel could tell Britney loved Kiana. She wagged her tail and whined.

"You're not allowed in here," Kiana said. "You know that. Back upstairs." She squeezed her snout gently and gave her a hug and a few scratches behind her ears. Britney yawned, licked her lips, then marched through the doorway and hopped up some stairs.

Lionel felt exhausted. "I thought she was really hurt," he said.

"You're so sweet," Gwen said. "Don't fall for her games. You're the boss. Next time give her a long walk. She needs to get used to walking again. Her master won't take her."

Binny bowed to her and grinned.

Gwen pursed her lips and looked at the doorway. "I had an idea while you were walking her, just an idea, but if any of you would like to make a little money, I could use your help with something, a part-time job, for a week or so — to finish what a certain someone has promised to do for years." She gave Binny a stern look.

Binny's smile faded. "Whatever I was supposed to do, I'm sure I had a great reason why I didn't do it — probably because all I do is work."

"Thanks for the coffee, Binny," the customer said. "See you tomorrow, Gwen." He left.

Gwen grunted at Binny. "We have a room upstairs, which we've always wanted to rent out to big groups for special events. Right now it's Britney's room, and it's so stuffed with junk we can't even ..."

"Hardly junk," Binny said. His eyes had lost their life, and he stood stiffly, arms across his chest. "There are a ton of valuable, very valuable items, things I've collected for this place for a renovation. And I've told you I'll get to it, once I finish the designs and ..."

"It's been six years," Gwen snapped. "Those designs must be incredible."

Kiana held her smoothie with both hands. Her body had tensed up, her lips pressed together.

Binny shook his head. "I should dry those glasses," he said, turning to the sink. "I've got no problem with you organizing stuff, but don't throw anything out. There's a fortune upstairs. I don't want to waste it." He flushed deeply and began to dry the glasses with a white towel.

"I don't want to throw out the important things either, dear," Gwen said softly.

Binny's shoulders relaxed and he slowed his drying. "It might be a good idea to organize things into sections; that would help me ... and I know I've taken too long."

"Exactly. We'll put all the dishes in one area, the kitchen stuff in another. You know I love some of those dishes you bought. They'll look so beautiful in here," she said wistfully. "Binny is the king of the flea markets; we've got enough stuff to build four cafés." She looked tired. "Anyway, I'd happily pay you guys to organize the stuff, maybe clean up a bit too, and … that would be a great help, and you could make a little money."

"I'd be happy to," Deepak said.

"Afonso?" Gwen asked the other boy.

"Sure, why not?" he said. "How much can you pay?" He took a slurp from his smoothie.

Gwen laughed. "That's what I like about you, Afonso. You get right to the point. How about ten bucks an hour?"

"Sounds good," Afonso said.

Did she mean him too?

"You boys aren't too busy at school?" Binny said. He was drying the inside of a glass furiously. "Lionel's got his running, and taking Britney for a walk."

So, he was included. It would be cool to earn some more money. He could buy that new controller.

"It's only for a week," Gwen said. "How about Monday after school? Can you boys make it?" Gwen said.

"Whenever you want," Deepak said. "I don't have anything after school on Monday."

"I can do it, too," Kiana said.

"I'm good Monday," Afonso said.

Lionel nodded weakly.

"Let's do it," Gwen said.

Binny wiped another glass. He wasn't keen on this. Kiana even looked a little scared. As soon as Gwen mentioned the upstairs, the three of them had gotten angry with each other.

Without warning, Binny spun around and looked hard at Lionel. "Are you running tomorrow?" he said. "We only open at ten."

"I was going to …" He usually slept in on Sundays. "I can wait until then and take Britney for her walk — if she recovers in time."

He surprised himself with that joke. It just popped out.

"Give her a good, proper walk, even if you have to drag her. Got it?" Binny winked. He sounded like his old self.

"Can I get you a smoothie?" Gwen asked Lionel.

This was his chance to leave. Kiana and the boys seemed like buds — and they were probably a little freaked out that they had to work with him on Monday. He'd figure out an excuse not to show — get sick or something.

"Thanks. I gotta get going. I have to help my mom with stuff," Lionel said.

"Another time," Gwen said.

"See you tomorrow," Binny said.

"Take care," Kiana said.

Deepak and Afonso said goodbye too, and Lionel left. The extra money would've been nice. That controller was getting on his nerves.

Without knowing why, he began to run back to his apartment. He didn't even feel the blister.

The shoes did feel awesome.

## Monday: 8:00 a.m.

Lionel held his breath, and then slowly unclenched his jaw. The dull pain in his head had become a thundering, pulsating nightmare of a headache.

"Mom! How stupid can you be?" he thundered.

He thought his head would explode. His mom, literally the messiest person in the world, who left her junk everywhere, had thrown out his old shoes this morning because he'd gotten those new joggers.

She wanted him to wear fluorescent green shoes to school? It's like she wanted him bullied.

His mind was reeling. He had to lean against the wall. Nick and Bryan and Mohamed would be playing football with his new shoes. He'd have to come home barefoot, and then he'd have to lie to Gwen and ...

He pressed the sides of his head as hard as he could. He needed to feel outside pain to stop the pain inside. He had to find his old shoes. He put the new ones on and went downstairs to the outside garbage bin. It reeked. No choice. He climbed in. For a second he thought he was going to be sick. He began to toss bags to the side.

Everything looked the same.

He began ripping bags open frantically. This was impossible. They could be anywhere. For ten minutes he kept looking, and with each passing moment, his anxiety got worse. He closed his eyes, panting hard.

"Please be a nightmare and let me wake up," he said to himself.

He opened his eyes. He was standing in a garbage bin. The nightmare was his life.

He was going to be late for school, and then Ryder would go nuts again and call his mom and make his life hell. He climbed out and went back upstairs to get his bag. He then hurried back to the street and ran as fast as he could to the bus stop.

His shirt was wet at the back and under his pits. He took off his backpack. He'd need to sneak into the washroom to clean up and use more deodorant. Luckily, the bus came about a minute later, but then he had to spend a terrifying twenty minutes with two girls sitting across from him. They were giggling the entire way — no doubt at his shoes.

Of course, he had to have English, with Nick and Kiana, so he was humiliated first thing in the morning. He made sure he was first in line, and as soon as the school doors opened he ran up the stairs and sat at his desk before anyone else. He tucked his feet under his chair and covered them up with his backpack. Hopefully, no one would notice. Once class was over, he'd fuss with his binder and be the last out. He sat at the back in science class so he could go in late and no one would see him. Then he had math. That meant more Nick.

His legs began to cramp up. Awesome — thanks life!

Too much running on the weekend. Stupid to run again Saturday night, and twice on Sunday, plus a long walk with Britney. Three times she'd flopped to the ground and began whining. He'd ignored her and each time she popped back up after five minutes and they kept going. She actually made it for a whole hour. Binny couldn't believe it and made a big fuss and gave him a strawberry-mango smoothie.

"Lionel, I'm not used to seeing you so prompt."

Mr. Whellan walked in. He wore a track suit. Whellan was the coach of the track and field team, so sometimes he wore that when they had a practise after school.

Lionel lowered his head and shrugged.

Whellan took a deep breath. "Is there any chance you finished your story?" he said.

Coming early was a brain-dead move. Better to sneak in when the class was about half full. No one would pay attention to him — they never did. He'd do that for math. He just needed to keep track of Nick.

"Sorry. I forgot it at home."

Whellan nodded a few times. "Yes, that can happen — certainly." He paused. "How about this, Lionel? I won't bug you about the story again, and when you remember to bring it, tell me, and you can read it to me after school one day instead of in class. Okay?"

Lionel couldn't believe his luck. He'd been dreading having to read his story for the past month — even thinking of it made his stomach queasy — and now it was over, just like that. He kept his eyes glued to the back of the chair in front of him.

"But understand I'm going to have to give you a zero if you don't get the story done, and I don't want to do that," Whellan continued. "So please make the effort, and I'd be happy to help you get started if you're having trouble coming up with an idea. Just ask. We could even meet after school today."

Kids began filing in.

A zero was the least of his problems. Teachers were so clueless about what really mattered at school.

"Thanks, Mr. Whellan. I'll try to remember to bring it next class."

"I'm looking forward to it," Whellan said.

"What're we doing today?" Rashmi said, as she took her seat.

Lionel could've hugged her for distracting Whellan.

"Your favorite subject," Whellan said. "Grammar."

A few kids booed.

"Now, now, grammar is your friend," Whellan said. "Think of it as a tool, a writing tool. It simply gives you some rules to help make it easier to express yourself. You use grammar all the time when you speak, all of you; you just don't realize it. The grammar we use to write may be a bit trickier, but once you learn it, you'll have a tremendous gift — you can express yourself easily, in different styles, too."

The entire class was soon seated. Lionel risked a quick look around. No Nick!

The air slowly seeped out of him. The basketball game! He'd mentioned it after gym class in the change room. Huge break — massive. He took a risk and stretched his right leg out slowly and massaged under his thigh, and then the same with his left. Maybe he could go for another run tonight. This running thing was strange. He liked it even though it hurt. He didn't worry about stuff when he ran — and his chest and stomach didn't hurt, and it was something to do other than game.

Whellan was explaining a grammar rule on the chalkboard, something about why you shouldn't write *is because*. He looked out the window. Dark clouds had rolled in. His run might be rained out. Too bad. He looked out again. But why not run in the rain? He wasn't gonna melt. Some kids held up their hands. Whellan must've asked a question. He picked up his pen and started to write the alphabet out. This was a classic trick of his. Teachers never asked you a question if you were writing something. One time for fun he wrote out the alphabet two hundred and fifty times in one class. The teacher didn't ask him a thing.

A folded piece of paper landed in front of him. His chest pain roared back. Someone had noticed his shoes. Stupid to think he was safe because Nick wasn't here.

This was only the start. Someone would snap a picture and Tweet it. He wanted to kill Gwen and Rajeev — and his mom.

He knew the entire class was waiting for him to read the note, waiting for him to get upset, tear up, look around in fear with that begging look bullied kids have, the look that said, "Just leave me alone — pick on someone else." That wasn't going to happen, though. He knew what to do.

Still as a rock, his eyes deadened and soft, he slowed his breathing and let his shoulders slump, quieting his thoughts until his brain was still, empty, smooth. He'd disappear. He'd done it so many times it was like second nature.

No reaction.

Keep calm.

Feel nothing.

He opened the note.

Lionel,

Heard that you got Brit to walk for a whole hour yesterday! And so nice of you to carry that brat all the way back to the café. You're sweet. See you after school for the big cleanup.

Kia

He met her eyes before he could stop himself. She smiled and flicked her eyebrows a couple of times. He nodded and turned away quickly.

"So, who can see the mistake in this sentence?" Whellan said, jabbing the board with his chalk.

Rashmi, Angelina, and Kiana raised their hands. Whellan pointed to his left. "Stephane, what do you think?"

"The pronoun doesn't agree with the verb," Stephane said.

"Right you are," Whellan said. "Good work. That's a tricky one. Who else saw that?"

A few kids put up their hands.

Lionel looked down at the note.

*See you after school.*

He couldn't actually go. He didn't know those boys. On the other hand, any excuse he came up with now would be lame. Kiana could see he wasn't sick — and she knew he wasn't sick yesterday. He was trapped. She'd know he'd chickened out if he didn't show, and she'd tell Nick.

He got an idea. He'd show up, stay for ten minutes, and then fake a phone call from his mom and tell them he had to go. They'd buy that.

His idea calmed him down, but his chest and stomach still hurt. This was going to be the longest day ever.

## Monday: 3:39 p.m.

Lionel crossed the street to the bus shelter. The bus must've just left — there was no one waiting. He'd run as fast as he could. Probably missed it by ten seconds. No telling when the next would come. Gwen would say don't worry, but he knew she'd be mad he was late the first day.

He leaned against the glass of the bus shelter. He tried to close his eyes and calm down. Kiana didn't want him there. She was just being nice with that note. He should be happy today was over and he could go home. It had been a miracle day: an insult-free day with clown shoes on. Funny that no one had said a word to him, like he really was invisible.

He'd find stuff at home to tone the green down. Hopefully,

by tomorrow, kids wouldn't even know they were green — and he'd be able to breathe again.

For ten minutes he watched the traffic whizzing past. A truck rumbled by, and behind it — the bus! Lionel hopped up the stairs.

"Hey, it's the Sorry Dude," the driver said.

"You're early today," Lionel said.

The doors closed and the bus set off.

"Not really, young man." The driver looked at his watch. "I'm maybe a minute ahead."

How'd he get here so quickly? Sure he ran — but that fast?

"I may look powerful, but I don't control time, bud. It marches on — too quick if you ask me. I used to be beautiful." He glanced at Lionel. "That was a joke, by the way."

"Sorry," Lionel said. "I ran from school and … I'm a bit tired."

"So, tell me. What's your name again?" the driver said.

"Lionel."

"Hi, Lionel. Bit better than the Sorry Dude, don't ya agree?"

"I guess."

"So, Lionel, those are some sick runners. What's your distance?"

"Um, I run, yeah."

"Must be a distance runner with those puppies."

"I'm a …" The driver wouldn't believe a fat kid like him ran for real. "I jog a bit, once in a while."

"Don't laugh," the driver said, "and I know you'd never believe a slob like me ran once, but I did tons of track in high school. Pretty good, too."

"What event?"

A few passengers filed by.

"The four hundred mostly, and a bit of eight hundred, and long jump." He sighed. "I blame Father Time. You blink and the next thing you know you're sitting on your butt ten hours a day and you're fat and outta shape." He patted his stomach and laughed, but this time he didn't sound happy.

"You could always start again. Running, I mean," Lionel said. "I just started running, to be honest. That's why I got these." He kicked a foot up.

"Run again? Do I look like a runner?"

"Not sure — I guess so. What does a runner look like, anyway?"

He laughed again. "I like you, Lionel. You're a cool kid, I can tell. And dammit, why not? I'm gonna get me a pair of fancy runners like you and hit the streets, and I'm gonna stop eating so much garbage. My wife's on me about it all the time. I don't need to eat a dozen donuts every morning, do I?"

"That might be a few too many."

They burst out laughing together.

"What do you have going on after school?" the driver asked.

"Not much."

"I bet you're meeting some buddies, right? I know kids hate telling adults what they're doing." The driver grinned and nodded a few times.

Lionel didn't want to sound like a total loser. "I'm sorta going off to work. I'm helping a friend … Well, I'm helping to organize some stuff … cleaning the second floor of a café."

The driver pulled over. It was Lionel's stop. The doors opened.

"Then you'd best get going, Lionel. Don't wanna be late for work — and when you see me next, we'll be fellow runners." He held out a thumbs-up.

Lionel flashed one back and left; just like that he decided to go to the café and work — and earn that money for the new controller. He didn't need to talk to anyone. Just work.

His new-found courage faded quickly as he got closer. He stood out front for a minute, his heart racing a million beats a second. He thought about that controller — he couldn't keep

using it. He had to kill those stupid skeletons already, and he
hated that ogre. He also didn't want to lie to the driver. If he saw
him tomorrow he'd ask how work went. Lionel was lying too
much lately.

He went inside. His heart was still pounding, but his chest
had stopped hurting and his stomach didn't feel its usual sick self.
Georgina was behind the counter. She'd gone hard-core Goth:
all black, fierce, ears covered in piercings, and the nose and
tongue too. The bangles and bracelets, which covered both wrists
and went halfway up her forearms, clinked as she came over.

"Are you Lionel, by any chance?" Georgina said. It was the
first time she'd ever spoken to him.

Flustered, he managed a nod. She had a pretty smile.

"Go right on up. Gwen's waiting for you," she said.

"And Binny?"

"Don't think so," she shrugged.

On a whim, Lionel took the stairs two at a time. He pushed
a heavy wood door open and stepped into a large room. The
right wall was lined with four tall windows looking out over
the street. They reached practically to the ceiling. The other wall,
which faced the back alleyway, had smaller windows. The ceiling
had wood beams running the entire length of the room, and
the floor had the widest wood planks he'd ever seen. Close by
the door, Britney lay on a thick area rug with a bowl of water at
her side.

Overcome by dust, Lionel sneezed.

Gwen whirled around, startled. Kiana stepped out from behind
a pile of boxes. Britney opened her eyes, let out a whimper,
and closed them again.

"You're right on time — even early," said Gwen. "Thanks.
The other boys should be here soon. Now that you've seen it, do
you still want to do it?"

Gwen looked sad. Only then did Lionel notice the mess: the broken furniture, the boxes, lamps, equipment, signs, and bits and pieces of metal parts and tools.

He'd cleaned his room. He could help fix this.

"It won't be that bad once we get into it," he told Gwen.

"There's a garbage bin in the lane behind the building, where we park," Gwen said. "You can toss the stuff that's broken or can't be used in there."

"Dad didn't want stuff thrown out, just organized," Kiana said.

"We won't throw out the good stuff," Gwen said, her voice strained. "But your father wants to rent this space out as a party room. When he gets back from visiting Grandma, he can figure out what we can use downstairs." She looked out the big windows overlooking the street.

"There are lots of nice things," Kiana said. "We should just organize it first."

Gwen ran her hand over a chair. The seat was missing. "It wasn't supposed to be like this ..." She broke off and gave her head a shake. "Well, I'm not helping, am I? I've been thinking you could make two piles: stuff you think has value and stuff you're not sure about. If something is absolutely broken and can't be used ... we can dump that into the bin. Make sense?"

The sound of feet stomping up the stairs interrupted her. Deepak and Afonso came in. Deepak rubbed his hands together and looked around, his head nodding.

"We'll have this place in shape in no time," Deepak said. "I have it all figured out, and I brought my computer so we could check the value of things online. He screwed up his eyes and put his computer down. "We'll put the good stuff in the far corner so it won't get wrecked. The maybe pile could be there against that wall. The junk ... the broken junk ... we can put it ..."

"My mom has a bin in the laneway," Kiana said.

"Excellent," Deepak said, rubbing his hands together. "Don't worry about anything, Gwen. By tomorrow, you won't recognize the place. I promise."

"Where's Binny?" Afonso said.

"He's visiting my grandmother," Kiana said.

"Binny's mom got ill, and he went to see her," Gwen said.

Gwen was usually so fun and full of energy, but every once in a while, when he wasn't expecting it, Lionel caught a glimpse of a sad face, like she was disappointed with something important, like she wanted to give up. He knew that face. It's how he felt most times — wanting to give up because there's no point and nothing is going to get better, and nothing is going to make guys like Nick less scary or take the chest tightness away, other than pills.

"You sure you want to pay us for this?" Afonso said. "This will take a long time."

"I absolutely do," Gwen said. "If you need anything, just come down."

She left.

"There's a ridiculous amount of stuff here," Afonso said. He pulled a chair off a pile of furniture. "I think there are like ten more chairs here, all broken. Is everything here junk?"

"No," Kiana said quickly. "Like Deepak said, we should make three piles ..."

"It's going to be a lot of work to carry this broken stuff down the stairs to the bin in the back," Afonso said.

"That's why she's paying us," Deepak said.

Afonso sniffed the air. "It's hard to breathe up here."

"It's just a little dusty," Kiana said.

"Should we start with the broken and useless stuff?" Afonso said.

"It's not useless," Kiana snapped. "Some of it got broken — from being up here so long."

Britney lay on the floor on her side and spread out her legs.

Deepak laughed. "You're not going to get any money if you act like that, Britney," he said.

Deepak rubbed her tummy. Britney grunted and closed her eyes.

Lionel wandered over to the window. Afonso was right. It was dusty. The back of his throat tickled. He looked down. The bin was directly below.

"Should we start at the back and work our way to the front?" Afonso said.

"Let's just start," Kiana said.

Kiana seemed irritated. Lionel felt the phone in his pocket. Maybe he should fake a call and get home.

"I was probably a little optimistic about finishing tomorrow," Deepak said.

"Or this month," Afonso said.

"Don't say that," Kiana said.

She sounded desperate. Lionel wondered why she cared so much. Afonso was right. Most of it was junk. He opened the window halfway to let in a breeze.

"Think of this as training," Deepak said to Kiana. "Don't you guys run up and down hills to build your muscles? We'll go up and down the stairs a few hundred times and soon we'll be ripped."

Afonso picked up two chairs. "If we're going to do this, then let's get to work."

Lionel pushed the window open completely. The opening was fairly big. He leaned out and looked at the empty bin below.

Afonso headed to the stairs, Deepak behind him. Kiana sighed and pulled two chairs from the pile. She looked over.

"Afonso is right. This stuff is broken and useless — and it'll take longer than a month," she said.

Lionel swallowed heavily. "There could be some good things," he managed.

She picked up the chairs. "Maybe. Take a couple chairs and let's go."

He looked down at the bin.

"I think we can throw stuff out this window."

Kiana blinked a few times, unmoving.

"The bin. It's right below us," Lionel said, barely louder than a whisper.

Kiana put the chairs down. "Let me see." She came over and looked out. Her eyes came alive and she laughed. "You deserve a gold star for this," she said. "Wait a sec."

She ran back to the chairs. Lionel wasn't sure exactly where she expected him to go. He looked out the window. Deepak and Afonso were beside the bin.

"One, two, three," Deepak sang out, and he threw a chair into the bin.

Afonso tossed his in next. The chairs rattled around noisily.

Kiana leaned her head out again. "Hey boys, how's the training going?"

They looked up.

"Better than yours," Deepak responded. "What's up?"

"Watch and learn," Kiana said.

She picked up a chair. The seat fell off. She laughed and then threw the frame out the window. Lionel watched it bounce around in the bin.

Deepak was ginning like mad. "So you've proven that you're smarter than us. So what? We're idiots."

He held out his fist and Afonso punched it. Kiana flung the chair seat Frisbee-style.

"Lionel thought of it," Kiana said. "Now get your lazy butts up here and let's get tossing."

Lionel got the last two chairs.

"Your idea. Toss away," Kiana said.

Lionel put them down. "You should do the tossing. I'll grab some more stuff for you."

It seemed like a boy thing to say, which was dumb because she was probably stronger than him. He scooped up a few chair parts that had broken off. This was firewood, not furniture. Binny would feel better when it was gone, for sure, like he had after he'd cleaned his room. He dumped the chair pieces by the window and went back.

Crash! Clang! Smash!

Kiana kept tossing things out. Lionel heard Deepak and Afonso tromp up the stairs.

"Let the mayhem begin," Deepak said.

Afonso looked into a big cardboard box. "This is full of old newspapers. What's your dad saving this for? Everything's online anyway."

Kiana threw the last of the furniture bits out the window. "Not sure. Maybe we should save it."

"Save it for what?" Afonso said.

Kiana shrugged helplessly.

Deepak looked in. "No one needs this, and the newspaper is all yellowed. He obviously isn't going to use it. It's been here for a long time." He put his arms around the box. It didn't budge. "This weighs a thousand pounds. How can paper weigh so much?"

"I'll help," Lionel said. He put his hands under the bottom and lifted it up. It wasn't that heavy, he thought.

Deepak began laughing. Lionel felt his face grow hot. He'd taken the box from Deepak.

"I think you can handle it," Deepak said. "I'll look for any boxes of feathers." He looked into the next box. "More news-papers. Afonso, come help. I'm too weak."

Lionel carried the box to the window, confused and not a little scared. Deepak didn't sound angry about it, but he couldn't be sure. This whole thing was becoming a huge stress.

"Toss it straight out," Kiana said.

Lionel rested the box on the window sill, closed the top so the papers wouldn't fly out, and tossed it out.

*Thump*.

A chair exploded as the box thudded on top.

"Cool!" Deepak said. He and Afonso were carrying another box together. "Let's keep crushing."

"We'll go for that guy in the corner," Afonso said.

"One, two, three," they said together and let the box fly. It hit the side of the bin and nicked a chair leg.

"Brutal," Afonso said disgustedly.

"Lionel, you throw the next one," Deepak said.

"Throw what?" Kiana said. She was carrying a shower rod.

"Lionel is the King of the Chair Crushers," Deepak said. "Get another box."

Lionel picked up another one. His hands shook slightly as he rested it on the window sill. They were setting him up. He'd miss and then the nicknames would come: King of the Chair Missers, Fattest Chair Thrower Ever, Tubby the Chair Tosser.

"Crush it, crush it, crush it," Deepak and Afonso chanted.

There was a chair close to the middle. That was an easier target. He threw the box.

"Yeah, baby!" Deepak roared. "That's how it's done."

Lionel looked on in amazement — a direct hit.

"Gwen's paying us by the hour," Afonso said. "Let's get going."

One after another the boxes flew out the window, followed by bottles, tiles, broken furniture, plates and dishes, three doors, one of which had a big hole in the centre, rotten floorboards, and a wooden barrel without a bottom. Deepak and Kiana kept up a steady conversation, with Afonso adding a comment here or there. Afonso was kinda funny, actually.

"We should take a quick break," Deepak said. "Afonso's tired."

He pulled out a chair from a pile of furniture against the wall and sat down. The back legs gave way and Deepak tumbled to the floor. Kiana and Afonso exploded in laughter. Lionel put a hand in front of his mouth.

Deepak remained stretched out on the floor. He looked hurt — badly.

Then Deepak began laughing, harder than Kiana or Afonso. "My spaghetti arms are so tired, I don't think I can get up."

"That looks comfy," Afonso said. "Let me join you."

Afonso pulled a chair out and sat down. "Great, the only chair that isn't broken," he said.

He jumped up and down a few times — until the back legs gave way and he fell beside Deepak.

"You gotta try it, Kia," Deepak said. "This floor is soft like butter."

"I'll try sitting the old-fashioned way," she said. Kiana sat in front of them, and they formed a circle.

There was no room for Lionel, but that was okay. They were friends. Lionel wandered to the back, picking through the various pieces of furniture, boxes, and piles of random stuff. There was still a lot of work to do, but he couldn't believe the change already. The area in front of the first two windows looking over the street had been cleared, letting light pour in.

"I bet we're going to fill another bin," Deepak said.

"At this rate we'll fill three or four," Afonso said.

Something caught Lionel's eye — a round tube, pinkish,

twinkling in the sunlight. It poked out from under a table with boxes stacked on top.

He moved the boxes. The table was actually nice, round with a marble top — at least he figured it was marble because it was cold to the touch. He liked it. It had that antique look. This might actually be their first keeper. He looked under the table.

The round tube was part of a chandelier. There were eight rounded glass tubes that narrowed into glass rose-shaped petals with tiny light bulbs. The sunlight from the window hit the glass, and red, pink, and yellow reflections danced wildly on the floor. The tubes were so delicate it looked as if the light bulbs were floating. He was afraid to touch it, and when he finally picked it up, he almost dropped it. How could something made of glass be so heavy?

"Bro, come take a break," Deepak called out.

The silence hung in the air. He had to say something.

"Sorry. I … It's just that I saw … There's this table, and I wanted to check it out. It's nice, maybe marble, the top, I mean, of the table — is marble. There's also a light fixture. I think it's a chandelier." He held it up.

He sounded like an idiot, as always.

They came over anyway.

"I knew there was good stuff in here," Kiana beamed.

Lionel held on for dear life. He didn't want to drop it. Kiana took one of the glass prisms in her hand.

"I bet this is worth something," she said.

"This calls for some investigation," Deepak said. "Let me fire up the computer."

"Lionel's right about the table," Afonso said. "That's a solid marble top, and in good condition. My dad used to fix things for people. He had a workshop at home. He used to fix lots of stuff — usually not furniture, more like machinery and old clocks.

He has a knack for figuring out what's wrong with things. I helped him too, polishing and putting things together."

The chandelier was getting heavy. Lionel felt the sweat gather at the back of his neck. He needed to put it down.

Kiana looked into his eyes.

"Maybe you should put it over in the far corner," she said, her lips curling upwards.

"Okay, if you want," he said.

"Need any help?" Afonso called out.

"I'm good," Lionel said. He gently lowered the chandelier to the floor and moved a couple of boxes around it to protect it. That's when he noticed a large, gray machine pressed up against the back wall. He had no idea what it was. A light green plaque on the front had a crazy name on it: Emmerich Maschinenwerke. Looked interesting. No way they could throw this puppy out the window. How did Binny even get it up the stairs?

"Hey guys, look at this," Deepak said. "That lamp might actually be worth something, unless I'm spacing out. It might be Italian, and if that's real glass, it's worth thousands."

While Kiana and Afonso went to see, Lionel kept looking around. Doorknobs, keys, locks, tools, wires, nuts and bolts, hangers, exit signs, old fuses, it was mostly all junk. Near the back he noticed a dingy screen with four sections. It was so dirty that he had another coughing fit when he touched it, and the tips of his fingers turned black. The frame was made of solid wood, dark, very smooth, and there was a thin inlay running along the sides of each section, in white, like ivory, and in each corner the line formed a star pattern. He folded it up and put it in the Maybe pile.

"How are you making out?" he heard Gwen say.

Her voice trailed off. She covered her mouth with both hands. Lionel shrunk back into the corner, glued to the floor, heart thumping. They'd done something awful. She didn't want them to throw out so much. Kiana had tried to tell them. Gwen looked about to cry.

"Looks ten times better already, doesn't it?" Deepak said.

"Once we moved the stuff from the window it got way brighter," Afonso said.

The color slowly came back to Gwen's cheeks and her eyes brightened. "I can't believe how much progress you've made. You're good workers."

Lionel had to gasp for breath. He'd been holding it in.

"Hey Lionel," Kiana called out. "Show Mom that light fixture, the glass one."

He held it up.

Gwen rushed over. "It's so beautiful. I never knew we had something like that. I can't believe it. Wow! I love it. I totally love it." She peered at it closely.

"I was looking at some websites. If it's glass, it could be worth a ton of money," Deepak said.

"I think it's definitely glass," Lionel said, "although it weighs a lot."

"Put it down and I'll take a closer look when I have a chance," Gwen said.

Lionel put it back in the corner.

"Did you find anything else worth keeping?" Gwen said.

No one answered. Her face fell. Lionel felt sorry for her. This room had a bizarre effect on her and Kiana, like a fast-acting sad pill. They both looked so happy when he'd shown them the chandelier. Probably didn't want to believe Binny only collected junk. He remembered the table.

"This table is pretty cool," Lionel said.

Gwen ran her hands over the top. "This is marble. Mister Binny, where did you get this?"

She obviously liked to see the keepers.

"There's a huge machine over there," Lionel said. "It looks like it's worth money."

"It's a coffee roaster," Gwen said wearily. "It's from Germany. Binny had this crazy idea to roast his own coffee and sell it. He was going to sell it all over the city ..." She looked out the window. "I'd forgotten about it. We had to take it apart to get it up the stairs, and still it took four men to carry the pieces." She took a deep breath. "It's getting late. We should call it a day."

Some stuff up here made Gwen and Kiana happy — other stuff made them sad.

"Do you think you might be able to get the roaster working?" Lionel said to Afonso.

Afonso ran his hands over the machine and peered all around. "I bet I can, with a little help from my dad."

"We could polish it up and make it look as good as new. Once we clean this place up, Binny can start roasting his coffee," Deepak said.

Gwen grunted. "I wouldn't bet on it," she said.

Lionel glanced at Kiana. Her eyes were puffy, like she was about to cry. Then she pressed her lips together and straightened her shoulders.

"I think we should at least try to get it working," Kiana said. "Do you really think you can?"

Afonso shrugged. "Don't see why not. It doesn't look complicated. Can my dad come tomorrow and take a look?"

"Of course," Gwen said. Her face softened. "Thanks again, everyone. Here's your pay. You sure earned it." She held out three twenty dollar bills.

Lionel took his. If they worked to the end of the week, he'd have that new controller, with money to spare. He put the money in his pocket.

"Sorry, but I have to miss tomorrow," Deepak said.

"That's fine," Gwen said. "Kiana has track practise and she can't come either. Are you two okay?" she asked Lionel and Afonso. "I'll order another bin."

Afonso said he could come. Lionel nodded. He figured that was his cue to leave.

"I should get going. Thanks," he said.

They said goodbye to him and he went downstairs. The café was quiet. A few customers were ordering at the counter. An old man was sitting at a table reading a newspaper. Georgina was making foam for a coffee drink. He didn't really know her, and he couldn't think of anything to say. He left.

Once the door closed, he felt bad. A simple goodbye wouldn't have killed him.

He put his hand in his pocket to feel the money. Twenty dollars! Stoked by the thought of a new controller, he began to jog slowly. He continued running all the way home.

## Monday: 6:25 p.m.

Lionel ran across the street, giggling to himself. Suddenly, he was running everywhere like a crazed dog! He heard something slam shut, like metal, and the good feeling disappeared. The Hombres were drinking. That meant trouble. He went a little faster.

"Hello there, Lionel."

Donna waved a big shopping bag. Lionel couldn't believe he'd mistaken her for a gangbanger! She'd been recycling.

"Have a good day at school?"

"School was okay. I … I got a job cleaning at a café, the second floor anyway — at Binny's Café. Do you know it? In the Market?

I made twenty bucks!" He took the bill from his pocket to show her.

A look of panic crossed her face. "Put that away," she whispered, pushing his hand down.

Too late.

"Bro, how 'bout loaning me some cash, huh?"

A thin, pale man, with dark circles around his eyes, wearing a ripped jean jacket and a bandana tied on one arm, came over slowly. His grin was cold and threatening.

Lionel stuffed the money in his pocket.

The man took a swig from a beer and held a hand out. "Help a brother out. I'll pay you back."

"It's ... not my money. I owe it to ..."

"I just need a loan," the man cut in. He laughed. "Give it over."

"We're just going inside," Donna said. "We don't want any trouble."

The man coughed violently and turned to spit on the ground. He stepped closer to Donna. "I don't want any trouble either."

Lionel held out the money. So stupid to flash money around. For twenty bucks the Hombres would break his arm — or worse.

The man chuckled and put it in his back pocket. He put his face close to Donna's. "See, no trouble, and everyone's happy," he said.

She kept her eyes to the ground.

"Ain't it getting past your bedtime, old lady?" he said.

Donna's lips pressed close together and she kept looking down.

Lionel's eyes burned and he wanted to knock the man to the ground.

Instead, he did nothing.

The man coughed a few times and spit on the ground. "I'll see you around," he said to Lionel, his eyes flashing. The man lifted his chin to them and walked off, staggering a bit.

"Let's go in," Donna said. She pulled him towards the front doors. "Be more careful."

He opened the door. "I'm sorry," he said. "I was being stupid."

She growled softly. "It's not your fault. I was on the verge of swatting him with this cane. If my son was here, that man would've been sorry."

Lionel had to laugh at the thought of Donna whacking the guy with her cane.

"I've learned not to come out at this time," she continued. "Those men like to drink on the basketball court before dinner — then they go who knows where. But I was so irritated with my neighbors. They won't recycle; they just won't. Last week I told them to pile their newspapers and bottles and pizza boxes by their door and I would recycle for them. I decided to do it before it got dark. Silly of me."

"You shouldn't be doing that for them." Lionel pushed the elevator button.

"I figured I'd do it once or twice and they'd feel guilty about me carrying their garbage, and then they'd take over." She scrunched her face up. "Not sure it's working. Five days later and I'm still at it. Breaking my back too. How many pizzas can you actually eat?"

He felt a pang of guilt. He and his mom never recycled. "I'll do it for you," he said. "Just leave the stuff by the door and I'll take it down. I run most mornings, so …"

The elevator opened and they got in.

"You've made my day, Lionel. You're such a nice boy — an example to some of them lazy kids who sit around playing video games or getting into trouble. I knew you were different the moment I met you."

"I'm not … that different."

"Don't be silly." She peered up into his eyes. "You're a good kid.

I can sense it. You're going to do great things in your life. Great things." The doors opened and they walked out. "Goodnight, Lionel, and thanks."

Lionel suddenly felt tired. He decided to eat and go to sleep, no gaming. He stepped into his apartment and stopped. The TV wasn't on. Usually, his mom was home by now. He sniffed the air — a weird lemony smell.

He looked around. He could see the top of the TV table — like, the entire thing, with nothing on it. No magazines, no papers, no cups, no dishes. The glass table top by the kitchen had a shine — the whole kitchen did, like it had been scrubbed.

He froze. He was in the wrong place — but the key worked? Lionel reached for the doorknob.

His mom came out of her bedroom. "Are you going out again?" she said.

He waved a hand in the air. "What's going on?"

She tucked a strand of hair under her bandana. "Your room looked so nice. I was so proud of how you organized everything that ... well ... I started feeling bad about how messy the rest of this place was. I gotta admit, I'm tired."

"That's how I felt and I only did my room," he said.

"That's because your room was extra messy," she joked. "Anyway, what d'ya wanna eat? The Sicilian?"

His stomach growled. He was ready for dinner, but he wasn't into pizza for a change. This was one weird day.

"Maybe we could make something, I don't know, a bit healthy, sorta? Nothing fancy, just not burgers or pizza; I'm kinda running a bit and I should maybe eat a bit better."

Her face fell. "I guess I could make something," she said. She put a hand over her eyes and rubbed them with her fingers. When she looked back up her eyes were red. "I think I should be apologizing for letting this place become such a pigsty — and for never cooking healthy food. That's not what a good mom does. I ... I dropped the ball; I let you down. Now you've started to exercise and I'm sitting in front of that stupid TV every night ..." She rubbed her eyes again.

"I didn't mean it that way, Mom. You shouldn't say that. We both needed to clean up. And maybe ... we shouldn't order in every night," he said. "Sure does smell good in here. Not so dusty."

"I'm gonna keep it that way."

"Me too."

"Deal."

She gave him a hug.

They looked at each other for a moment.

"So, Mom, do you know how to make things? For dinner, I mean?" he said.

She raised her eyebrows. "I'm not completely useless, Lionel."

"I didn't mean that."

She rubbed his arm. "No, you're right. When's the last time I cooked anything that wasn't microwaved or fried? But there was a time ... and I don't think I've forgotten everything. I could slip down to the supermarket. It's still open. I'll get something, maybe chicken, don't know, just something that's not frozen or junky. A runner needs his energy."

"Do you want me to come?"

She gave his arm a squeeze. "Thanks, but you relax. You've had a long day."

"So have you."

"I want to do it. I really, really do. I want to do this — for you." She took a deep breath. "But tell me. How did your job go? Today was the first day, right?"

"Great. I made twenty dollars." He didn't tell her what happened to the money.

"I'm so proud of you. I can't believe how awesome you've been lately. Of course, I can believe it because you're always awesome … but you know what I mean." She gave him another hug and kissed his cheek.

"You watch TV or game," she said, "and I'll be back soon to teach that kitchen some manners." She patted his arm, and then left with her purse over her shoulder.

He looked at the TV and the computer. He couldn't, not now; it felt wrong, like he'd be wasting his time being lazy — a Do-Nothing. He couldn't remember when he had such an over-whelming urge to move, as if his butt would burst into flames if he so much as sat.

He couldn't go for a run because his mom would be back soon. He tried to remember how many times he'd run lately. The first time was Saturday, or maybe Friday if he counted chasing that bus, although maybe that shouldn't count because he'd been so slow. Probably a good idea to keep track of his runs so he'd know for sure. He taped some notebook paper together and drew a calendar for the next three months, and then taped it to the wall over his desk in his bedroom.

He felt his stomach where his belly hung over his belt. He was so flabby and gross it was … gross. Marcus had been making them do sit-ups and push-ups as a warm up. He told them a real athlete needed a core of iron. Usually, Lionel faked them. He looked up at the sheets of paper. There was room at the bottom. He wrote *Exercises* under the calendar. He'd put a star for every day he did a hundred sit-ups and fifty push-ups.

Lionel figured he should do the push-ups first because they were harder. He lowered himself down. His arms shook and his stomach touched the floor before his nose. He hated his body.

Lionel got to five and felt his strength giving out. He managed a final one — and collapsed to the floor.

He did one more — and collapsed again. He pictured Nick laughing his face off.

He kept going, taking a rest every two or three push-ups. "Fourteen, fifteen, sixteen ..." he grunted out.

His iron core had a ways to go. Right now it was more like jelly.

He imagined his chart filled with stars and check marks — every day. A sea of them, from end-to-end.

"Seventeen, eighteen, nineteen."

And he imagined how he'd look — and who he'd be.

## Friday: 3:55 p.m.

Lionel walked into the café, not quite sure how he felt — both happy and sad. He'd gone hard at it Tuesday and filled another bin himself. Afonso had worked on the coffee roaster. On Wednesday, he filled another half a bin. Kiana missed Tuesday and came late Wednesday after her track practise. Deepak could only help Wednesday for an hour because of a piano lesson. When Lionel left on Thursday, Gwen told him he'd done an awesome job. Maybe he had — it sure didn't look like the same place.

He couldn't believe it was Friday already, and that explained the sadness. He liked working here, and not because of the money. He liked talking to Georgina and Gwen, and he liked listening to Deepak joking about everything, and Afonso was smart and a bit more serious like him. They both liked gaming, too. He'd even talked to Kiana a few times.

This had been a perfect week at school. No one had said a word to him: no teachers asked him a question, no kids bumped into him in the hall or chirped him. Nick had given him a few looks that scared him a bit, like he was suspicious of something. But Nick was acting weird with everyone. He was also hanging out with Kiana and Rashmi a lot more during recesses and lunch. It bugged Lionel that Kiana was with him, but at least Nick wasn't bullying anyone.

To top off the week, he had enough cash to get the new controller, and he could game all weekend and finally crush the skeletons and the ogre and those disgusting vultures.

"Lionel, looks great up there," Georgina said to him. "I can't believe it's the same place. You guys are amazing. There's lots of cool stuff, too."

"The keeper pile got pretty big, actually," Lionel said. "We found some dishes and coffee cups, and some old photos of people drinking coffee and tea in cafés all over the world."

Lionel especially liked the old pictures, and while sorting them he imagined living back then, in another country, on some other continent even — as another person.

"Afonso and Manuel got the old coffee roaster working too," Lionel added. "Manuel said it was over eighty years old. Apparently, Binny's gonna roast his own beans and sell them to restaurants or in grocery stores. That's the plan, anyway."

She smiled. At first, Georgina had freaked him out with her jet black hair and piercings and tattoos and leather boots, but they'd started saying hi to each other and then she brought him a smoothie a couple of times. When he left last night they talked for a good fifteen minutes.

She had two big dangling silver earrings engraved with skulls, which he'd never seen before.

"Where'd you find those?" he asked, pointing to the earrings.

"You're so sweet to notice. Aren't they amazing?" She gave them a twirl, and they swayed back and forth a few times.

"Very amazing," Lionel said. "I'll just head up. I think we're basically finished, depending on what Gwen wants to do with the keeper stuff. We have to sweep and organize a few things, and then we're done."

She pouted. "Does that mean I won't see you around?"

"I'm still walking Britney, so ..."

Her pout remained. "You have to promise to visit me, okay?"

He knew she was only being nice. Still, it wasn't too often

someone asked him to visit. Even a pretend invitation was better than no invitation at all. "I will. I only live down the street."

She began to clean some glasses with a cloth. "You'd better, or I'll be mad at you."

He waved and started upstairs. Half way up, he heard voices. Gwen was talking.

"... like I promised. Look. We kept the valuable things, what looked important."

"It was all important," Binny thundered.

Lionel stopped in his tracks.

"Where do some punk-ass kids get off throwing out a lifetime of collecting? Do you understand what they did? I had it all planned out. I had tiles, plans ... ideas — and now it's all gone, the dream is dead, wrecked. I can't believe you lied to me about my mom to get rid of me. I can't believe I fell for it."

"I didn't lie," Gwen said. "Your mom seemed upset and not feeling well and ..."

"Yeah, right. I can't believe you were part of this, Kiana," he continued.

Lionel felt so dizzy he had to grab the banister. Binny wasn't just angry. He was in a rage. Lionel's throat went dry. He sounded madder than Brent — than his dad. Binny would kill him if he went up there. He took a step back.

The stair creaked.

"Who's there?" Gwen called out.

He froze. Stupid old stairs. He waited a few moments, and then very slowly took another step back. He had to get away, and he'd never come back or even walk through the Market, not ever.

"Lionel, come on up."

Gwen was looking at him, her face grim and eyes tight. "Please. It's fine."

His throat was too dry to answer.

"It's okay, Lionel. Trust me," she said tenderly. "Please. We're just talking. That's all. Nothing to worry about, I promise."

She was obviously close to tears. He couldn't run away now. Kiana would know. He followed her into the room.

Binny spread his arms out. "The only thing you didn't throw out was Britney," he said.

"I wouldn't hurt Britney," Lionel said, his voice barely above a whisper.

"Dad, there were a lot of broken things ... but look at all the stuff we kept," Kiana said. Her cheeks were marked with tears.

"I'm looking. Not seeing much," Binny said.

"There's all this," Lionel said. His chest felt so tight he had trouble breathing. "The coffee roaster works. This chandelier could be worth a lot of money because it's glass, and Italian. There are those dishes over there, and that table ... and that screen. The floor's been cleaned ... and I think it looks good, with the wide boards and ... We found these pictures, and maybe you could use them — in the café?"

He had to stop. His throat had gone dry again.

"The space is so big and bright," Gwen said.

"We didn't throw out anything nice," Kiana said.

"We can hold parties up here, rent out the space," Gwen said.

"You can start roasting your coffee, like you planned," Kiana said.

"The chandelier is beautiful. It'll look amazing downstairs," Gwen said.

Binny held his hands up. "You can stop for a second." He cast a sorrowful look about. "Lionel, sorry for yelling. I know you wouldn't hurt Britney. It's just ... just ... I can't believe you threw out my stuff." He rubbed his chest with his right hand. "I swear my heart's gonna burst. It's like my ribs are crushing me. I'm serious. It's like I've been emptied out, like my entire life's been taken from me." He seemed helpless.

"I feel like that a lot," Lionel said to Binny. "I'm sorry. I just wanted to ... I thought you wouldn't want the stuff we threw out, like the newspapers and tiles, because a lot of the tiles were broken or not matching, and the papers were old and yellowy and they smelled kinda dusty. And some of the furniture wasn't really ... I mean you couldn't use it because it was broken; but maybe you could've fixed it and I didn't think of that, too busy being stupid."

He lowered his gaze, determined to say what he felt and then leave. This wasn't Kiana's fault, or Gwen's, or Deepak's or Afonso's.

It was his fault. He'd done most of the work.

"I know what you mean, that empty feeling," he continued. "It's like you know everyone else has something and you don't, and you don't even know what it is they actually have or how to get it. You just know you want it. For me, I'm always feeling tight, in my stomach, or my chest, or my head, like there's something pushing on me, and then for some stupid reason I cleaned out my room one night, got rid of some junk I had since I was a little kid, put away my clothes, even cleaned the floor — everything. And that night, I don't know why, the pushing and the pain went away. I felt like I was floating on my bed — for real — and that night I thought about why I felt so much better. I thought and thought until it just hit me: stuff is just that — stuff. Why keep stuff around if it doesn't make you feel good?"

Kiana was looking at him intensely. It unnerved him. He was making a fool of himself.

"I'm sorry," he said, his voice breaking. "I think I tried to do here what I did at home. Don't be mad at Kiana. She was at track a lot, and she tried to stop me. Afonso spent most of the time fixing the roaster, and Deepak ... he had a piano lesson. Gwen was more shocked than anyone when she saw it. I didn't listen, though. Every time I tossed something broken or old I felt better. I knew it wasn't mine. I did it anyway. It wasn't their fault. I picked most of the stuff to toss. I messed up — as usual."

For once in his life he wished he could say what he meant without sounding like an idiot — just once. He took a deep breath. The sadness in the room ripped at Lionel's heart; he could actually feel it, like a hook pulling him in.

A tear fell down his cheek. Kiana was crying too. Gwen rubbed her eyes.

"I know I have a problem with ..." Binny lowered his gaze. "This hoarding thing has taken over. Not sure when, not sure why. One day I woke up and I had a room full of broken, mismatched tiles and boxes of old newspapers."

Tears now fell freely down Gwen and Kiana's cheeks.

Binny's voice became distant and flat. "I'm the one who's made a mess of things. I'm the idiot who stuffed this place so full of junk he sucked the life from it. And now I'm acting like the biggest jerk in the world to a great kid like Lionel. Sorry, Lionel. No excuses. Please, forgive me."

Lionel stared at him. This made no sense. Forgive him for what?

Binny managed a smile, his sad eyes twinkling ever so briefly. "You're right. Most of that stuff, almost all of it, was garbage — busted, ugly garbage. I used to talk so much about using it to fix up the café that I even convinced myself that I was gonna do it. Once in a while the reality hit me and I'd get so scared and that empty feeling would get so big, I swear I thought it would swallow me up."

Lionel also knew what that was like.

Binny looked back to Gwen. "We had such plans, didn't we?

We were gonna make this place special; people were gonna come from all over, rich people, poor people, regular people, seniors, students — everyone — because it was so beautiful. We were even going to roast our own coffee. And what did I do? I spent years piling garbage into this room, obsessing over it, terrified by it. Beautiful? Binny's Café is a dump." He buried his face in his hands.

Gwen and Kiana walked over to him, their feet barely making a sound, just tiny squeaks, and he wrapped his arms around them. Lionel knew he should look away. He should give them some privacy. He couldn't tear himself away, though. He couldn't. For once in his life he was close to a real family, with people who cared for each other. It warmed him, filled him with a gentle heat, and he closed his eyes and felt another tear fall.

He didn't care if they saw.

"My new life begins today," Binny said. "I promise. I ain't slaving to a pile of garbage anymore. I can breathe better already, honest. I was so scared of not having this stuff, and now that it's gone, I feel ten times better, a hundred times. I feel free of it — and all it took was for Lionel to throw it out. Man, I'm ridiculous."

Binny had a crazy grin on his face, his eyes alive and dancing, and he took three strides and gave Lionel a bear hug. Lionel tensed involuntarily. Binny squeezed and wouldn't let go until Lionel relaxed his body and hugged him back.

"I knew there was something special about you," Binny said, letting him go. "I could tell. 'Here's a kid that's gonna make a difference,' I told myself. Well, you sure did! Look at this place. Amazing. I love it. Love, love, love it. Tomorrow we start. I promise. Out with the old and in with our new chandelier."

They turned to the stairs. Deepak and Afonso walked in, along with their dads.

## Friday: 4:05 p.m.

Rajeev rushed forward, stopped, and scanned the room.

"I am very much impressed," Rajeev said, head wagging side-to-side. "I most sincerely am. Truly. It is an utter transformation, nothing less. Something ugly, a mess, broken and battered, is now beautiful. These floors, the windows, this space — remarkable. I am even a bit overwhelmed … and not a little ashamed." He hung his head. "My store is a disgrace: chipped shelving, dust, dirty carpets, and the stockroom is a disaster. Most of the time, Deepak and I can't find the shoes for the customers." He took a deep breath and put a hand to his cheek.

"We could help you," Deepak said. "Maybe some new carpets and shelves? I don't know. But we could do something — even paint."

"Son, you are speaking wisely. We'll make old Mister Adler proud, yet." Rajeev turned to Lionel. "I understand you are the mastermind behind all this?"

"We all helped," Lionel stuttered.

Deepak waved him off. "Lionel did most of the work."

"Hardly," Lionel said. He collected himself. "I'd be happy to help you fix up your store."

"I would be delighted to work with you," Rajeev said.

"Me too," Afonso said.

"Don't forget me," Kiana piped in.

Binny took hold of Manuel's elbow and pointed to the coffee roaster.

"That's the craziest idea I ever had," Binny said. "I was going to roast my own coffee and use it for the café, and maybe even sell it around town. Had the bags designed and everything, even the name — Binny's Beans. Can't believe how much trouble I went to take it apart and haul it up here. I even had to put some metal joists under the floor to support it. Big dust collector is what it is. But you get major props for making her pretty."

"We did more than that," Afonso said. "My dad and I ..."

"It was all Afonso," Manuel said. "I just gave him some pointers and found the spare parts he needed."

Lionel had scrubbed it with special cream for twenty minutes yesterday to get it clean.

"She's almost as good as new," Afonso said. "Had to put in a new motor and fix the wiring, but otherwise it was in good shape. You can start roasting any time."

"Seriously?" Binny said.

"Try it out," Afonso said.

Binny hit the switch. The roaster began to hum, and the roasting chamber began to spin around.

"Let me pay you for the parts at least," Binny said, in a serious tone.

"You won't pay us anything," Manuel said. "On the other hand, if I were to receive a free pound of beans, perhaps I wouldn't object."

"You've earned yourself a free lifetime supply," Binny declared. He bounded over and shook Manuel and Afonso's hands.

Manuel cast a sideways glance at the roaster. "I'm kinda thinking like Rajeev here. My garage is a mess, tools all over, and the grease is so thick I leave every day covered in it. I have old tires I'll never use in a million years, and cans, and screws, and ... I could start my own landfill site."

"I could help you, too," Lionel said.

"I reserved his services first," Rajeev cried.

"I'll pay more," Manuel said, laughing.

"How have the jogging shoes worked out for you?" Rajeev asked Lionel. "I noticed you running past my store with Britney a few times."

Britney was sniffing around.

"He's in training," Binny said. "He's our Marathon Man."

"You're running a marathon?" Manuel said.

This was getting stupid. Did he look like a marathon runner? He had been running every day, often twice, and his wall was filling up with check marks and stars. He was up to five hundred sit-ups and a hundred and fifty push-ups a day. But that didn't make him a runner. He needed to put a stop to this before they found out the truth. "I don't run all that much," he said. "A few times a week, no big deal. No marathons."

"I have tried to encourage my Deepak to engage in more physical activity," Rajeev said.

"It's not your fault I'm lazy," Deepak grinned.

"You should run with Lionel," Gwen said. "You might not keep up, but it's a start."

"I'd be up for that," Deepak said.

Manuel elbowed Afonso. "Soccer is starting soon. Wouldn't hurt you to start training."

"Sounds good," Afonso said. "When do you run — mornings or nights?"

Lionel figured they'd be too busy to run in the morning. "I usually get up early and run in the mornings. Dumb habit, so ..."

"I'd love to run with you guys," Kiana said. "I maybe get two track practises a week. Whellan does so much at school he doesn't have the time."

"It's the morning, early. Are you sure ...?"

They weren't listening to him.

"It wouldn't hurt Britney to run either," Gwen said. "She's fat enough for two dogs, and she loves her walks with Lionel."

"We'll take you too, Miss Chubby-Wubby," Kiana said. She gave Britney a vigorous pet under her belly.

"You should name your running club," Rajeev said.

"Afonso and I can be the Slow Guys in Slow Motion," Deepak said.

"You're not building my confidence," Afonso said.

"It should be something about the Market," Kiana said.

"How about the Marketeers," Lionel said. The name just popped into his head.

"That is very clever," Rajeev said. "It combines the fact you all know each other from the Market with the sense of camaraderie in Alexandre Dumas's classic adventure story, *The Three Musketeers*."

They stared at him.

"You guys should read more," Kiana said. "I read that last year. Have you read it?" Kiana said to Lionel.

"Not yet," said Lionel. He hadn't read a book in years. "Is it good?"

"It's amazing," Kiana said. "I'll give it to you."

She sure seemed excited about this book. He said thanks to be polite.

"So, what time should we meet?" Deepak asked.

"How about seven?" Afonso suggested.

"Not much time for a shower before school," Kiana said.

"So, maybe six thirty?" Afonso countered. "Later on weekends, I suppose."

"I thought the Marketeers was gonna be fun," Deepak moaned.

"We need to celebrate the birth of the Marketeers in style," Manuel said. "Get your butts downstairs — and drinks are on me."

"No chance," Binny said. "You ain't making me look bad in my own place. You're all gonna rip me off and have your drinks for free."

Binny clapped Manuel on the shoulders and the two of them led the way. Lionel hung back, not wanting to get in the middle of things. As Gwen left, he decided to take a last look. It really was a beautiful space. He let himself feel a little proud of what he'd done.

The best part: Kiana's family was happy about it.

"You admiring your handiwork?" Kiana said.

He nearly dropped to the floor in shock. How come she wasn't downstairs? They were alone in the room — together!

"I ... um ... thought I'd forgotten something — but I hadn't."

"C'mon. If anyone deserves a treat, it's you."

"Okay. Thanks." This conversation needed to end. He took a step towards the stairs, but Kiana reached out and held him lightly by the arm. The touch of her hand sent a flash of heat up to his shoulder. He looked down at the floor, feeling so uncomfortable it was all he could do to stop himself from running off.

"I don't want you to think my dad's a hoarder like those freaks on TV. He's not. It's just, at least this is what my mom thinks, that my dad got into ... like ... a bad habit. He began to collect, and then collecting became way more important than what he was collecting, and then he began collecting things he shouldn't have and ..."

She was obviously struggling to explain something to him. Why him, though?

"I was happy to help."

She raised her arms and let them flop to her sides. "I'm never good at saying what I mean. I'm stupid that way."

"You're the smartest kid in school."

She blushed. "Not sure about that. There's a difference between school smart and life smart. Anyway, I wanted to tell you how awesome this is and ... it was fun getting to know you ... and talking to you. You're different at school. You never say anything." She laughed. "Just thanks, okay."

He'd never seen her look so beautiful. They sat close to each other in English, but this was different. She was actually talking to him. He'd clean ten rooms full of junk to share a moment like this. He looked fully into her eyes. He'd never done that before. They were crystal clear blue, soft and light, with a tiny bit of green around the edges. He wondered why he'd never noticed that green color before.

She was the first to look away. "You wanna ... um ... get down there? I'm dyin' for a mango-strawberry-banana smoothie."

"What do you want, Lionel?" Binny's voice rang out as they walked into the café.

They were sitting around two tables that had been pulled together.

"I'm okay, thanks," he said.

He didn't want to look like the typical fat kid who ate all the time — it was just nice to be included in the Marketeers. He'd also promised himself not to drink any pop until all the boxes on his running sheet were checked.

"Hey, Georgina, get Lionel something to drink, will ya?" Binny called out. "We can't have a toast unless everyone has a full glass. It's bad luck."

"Maybe I'll go pick something," Lionel murmured.

"Go for it," Binny said. "Anything you like."

"Can you get my smoothie?" Kiana said.

He nodded and went to the bar. Georgina was pouring beer from the tap into frosted pint glasses. He waited for her to finish.

"You need something?" she said. Her face was cold and her jaw set firmly in place.

She sounded irritated, almost mad, which wasn't like her, at least not with him. "It's Kiana. She wants a mango-strawberry-banana smoothie."

Her shoulders slumped and she put two beers and two orange juices on the counter. Somehow Kiana's order upset her. Probably because it was more work.

"I'll just have some water — and thanks."

A glimpse of a smile appeared. "Water? That's it? Binny's buying."

He nodded.

The smile got bigger. "Ice?"

"I guess. Thanks."

She began to put the fruit in the blender.

Lionel didn't want to just leave. It seemed unfair, with everyone getting a drink except her. "Did you hear that we're starting a running club?"

"I know. Binny told me."

"Do you run at all?"

She turned the blender on leaving him wondering if she'd heard, so he waited until she finished. It took a long time.

Binny was getting impatient. "Hey, Georgina, it's a smoothie," he called out. "You don't have to pulverize it for half an hour. I'm a thirsty man here."

"I'm coming," Georgina said gruffly, twisting the blender from the base.

"So, do you run?" Lionel said.

The question embarrassed her. "I don't anymore, not since I was a little kid in cross-country, like in grade three, and I'm a bit of a klutz."

"Me too," Lionel said, "but we're only jogging. It doesn't matter how fast you are. You can't be slower than me."

"You run all the time," she said.

As if.

"You should come," he said. "It's early, like six thirty in the morning, but it might be fun. We won't run too far, I bet, and like I said, I'm so slow you could keep up easy."

She picked up the tray. Lionel was amazed at how strong she was. The tray was loaded and she carried it like a pile of feathers.

Lionel suddenly got it. "Georgina's going to join the Marketeers," he said, following her to the tables.

"Lionel," Georgina hissed.

"For sure. The more the merrier," Deepak said.

"Get yourself a drink and get over here for the toast," Binny ordered Georgina.

"Well, I could use the exercise, I guess … on days I'm not opening," Georgina said quietly.

"I'm happy to open for you," Gwen said.

Georgina put the tray on the table. "Smoothie's for Kiana, right? I assume you two are having the beers." She gave them to Binny and Manuel. She gave Gwen and Rajeev the orange juice. "Here's your water," she said, holding it up for Lionel.

"Hurry up and grab something," Binny said to Georgina.

"I'm okay," she said.

"No chance. That's an order," Binny said.

Georgina blushed. "Thanks. I'll just have a Coke." She scurried back to the counter.

"You're having water?" Kiana said to Lionel. "You gotta live once in a while."

"I'm thirsty," he said.

"You sure you don't want something else?" Gwen said to him.

"This is fine," Lionel said.

Georgina came back with a Coke.

"We're ready," Binny declared. He held up his beer, and everyone else held up their glasses. "I want to thank you kids, and the beautiful Gwyneth, for cleaning up my mess. I feel so great I could almost join the Marketeers myself — almost."

They laughed.

"Thanks to Deepak and Kiana for all their hard work, and to Afonso and Manuel for fixing the roaster. Here's to Binny's Beans being a massive success, and here's to Rajeev and Manuel fixing up their places too, and most of all, here's to Lionel for doing most of the heavy lifting."

"To new beginnings," Gwen said, clinking her glass with Binny's.

"New beginnings!" the rest of them sang out.

Kiana held her smoothie towards him. Lionel gave it a touch.

A new beginning? It was something he'd dreamed about — for a very long time.


## Friday night: 6:35 p.m.

Lionel covered his mouth and looked down at the sidewalk as a group of girls walked by. He prayed they hadn't seen him laughing to himself, like he was some outpatient from a mental hospital. He couldn't help it when he remembered how Binny bet Georgina he could balance her Coke on his head — and it fell all over him. Binny laughed so hard Lionel thought he was gonna have a heart attack.

Weirdest part was, Lionel had the feeling Binny knew he couldn't do it, but tried anyway. Lionel would've been so humiliated he'd have run straight out and never come back. Binny wiped himself off and kept right on joking around with them. He even said he'd come out with the Marketeers one weekend, and that he was going to try and stop smoking — which made Gwen cry again.

Kiana — it still didn't seem real. They'd talked the entire time. Of course, he couldn't think of anything cool or funny to say, except it didn't matter because she asked him a million questions and told him about her teachers and how Ian had this crush on Rashmi and drove her crazy with ten texts a day, and that Rashmi kept saying to Kiana she didn't like him — she always answered to be polite, she said — which made Kiana think that deep down she did like him. Kiana also told him Nick was texting her a lot, and he kept asking to go to Pearl's for lunch or after school, and she'd kept putting him off until it was getting rude so she finally said yes.

The only negative was Kiana pressing him about his English story. She forced him to tell her about it; worse, she made him promise to let her read it. She even said it sounded awesome, which he couldn't believe was true. Then she told him she wanted to be a writer someday, and she made him promise never to tell anyone or she'd kill him because she was so embarrassed about it — as if Lionel had anyone to tell. Lionel said her story was the best in the class and he thought she'd be a great writer. After he'd said that, she took a long sip from her smoothie, like she was thinking about something important.

Lionel surveyed the front of his building. It looked like the coast was clear, and he didn't hear any music playing from the basketball court. No Hombres. He waited for a break in the traffic and then sprinted for the front doors. He hadn't seen that man since he'd stolen his money. Lionel wasn't taking any chances, though, and he made sure the Hombres didn't see him coming or going.

He felt a smile break out. It sure was nice to sit in the café and talk to Kiana. It didn't bother him that Kiana was doing it because she had to. Kids like Kiana know how to talk to someone like him. He'd seen it tons of times. Popular kids would treat losers nice once in a while, for no reason — because they could. The mistake was thinking the popular kid was your friend. Try doing that at school and Kiana would put him in his place. He got in the elevator and laughed out loud when the doors closed. Like they were going to be *besties*!

He stepped out. Three pizza boxes had spilled across the floor in front of the apartment next to Donna's. They really were pigs. He bent down to pick them up. He'd better run this downstairs to the recycling bin. A couple of days this week he'd been late getting back from the café and Donna had taken the recycling down. He'd felt guilty about that. She was too old to be lugging pizza boxes and bottles.

Donna's apartment door opened.

"Lionel, this is so nice. I was going to knock on your door and drop something off. Then I heard the elevator and thought it might be you."

Caught red-handed. "I was late today. Sorry. I was at the café and ... I'm sorry about this mess. I'll get these in the bin," he said.

"Those boxes can survive until tomorrow. Give them here."

"I ... I'm sorry. I'll do better next week."

She walked over to him. "Poor Lionel. Everything is hard for you, I think. Give me the boxes. You've had a long day. I'll put them out tomorrow morning and you can take them then. Okay?"

She reached her arms out and Lionel gave her the boxes. Suddenly, she threw her head back and laughed.

"You are the dearest young thing. So serious. What other teenager would be so worried about recycling pizza boxes?" She tapped her cane on the floor. "By the way, thank you for telling me about Binny's. I went there the other day and had a nice cup of coffee and a muffin, which was delicious, and I had a nice chat with a young girl who dresses like a witch."

He laughed. "That's Georgina. She's nice."

"She is, once you get past the horrible stuff she's done to

herself, what with those earrings everywhere and all those silly tattoos." Her eyes got wide and she took hold of his forearm. "She even has a pierced tongue! An earring right through her tongue. Yuck! I asked her why she'd do something so silly, and she said she liked the way it looked. I said no girl in her right mind would put an earring in her tongue. We had a good time, though. I like her. Anyway, how's the job going?"

"We're done. Afonso, one of the other kids, fixed a coffee roaster and Binny's gonna start roasting his own beans — Binny's Beans — like real gourmet coffee. He's gonna fix up the café with some of the stuff he's collected, like with a chandelier and pictures and plates, and now I'm gonna help Rajeev and Manuel fix up their places, so that's good — and we have a running club — the Marketeers."

"That's wonderful. Sounds like things are working out well." She looked at her watch. "You'll have to excuse me, though. I arranged to Skype my son. He's in California — an actor." She was obviously proud of him.

"I'm sorry. I didn't know. I'm sorry."

She rapped the floor with her cane. "You stop being sorry all the time," she snapped. "Honestly, you say sorry more than anyone I know — and I don't know what you're sorry about. Now can you be a sweetie and put those boxes in my apartment?"

Lionel followed her back. He looked in. Her place was neat and tidy.

"Just put them there," she pointed to a space under the table in her hallway. "Now, wait for a moment."

Before he could say a word, she disappeared into her bedroom. Moments later she came back. "Here you go. This is for helping me with my neighbors. I hope you like it."

He took the bag. "You didn't need to … It's not my birthday or anything, and I don't mind helping."

"Shush. I like buying presents for my friends. Now open it up. I have to make my call."

"It's one of those smart watches, I think they call it," she said. "Keeps track of your distance and your time and how many strides you take. It even tracks your heart rate, although I have no idea how it does that. The person at the store said it also lets you text and check emails ... You kids are so good with technology. I'm sure you'll figure it out."

"I can't take this. It's too much. And I'm not a runner — I mean, not really."

"I think you're a runner," she said softly. "Have a good night, dear. Come by and say hello tomorrow if you have a chance."

"Okay ... Bye."

He closed the door behind him and looked at the watch as he went to his apartment. He wasn't a runner. Okay, he ran and he liked it, but he wasn't like Kiana. Donna was right about one thing, though: he did say sorry all the time. Even before he began to talk to someone he somehow felt like he'd done something wrong, like he was gonna say something stupid and would end up feeling sorry in the end, so he should get it over with and say sorry up front.

His mom looked up from the kitchen table as he opened the door. "Lionel, where have you been? I was so worried. I've been ... I thought you were coming home from school. You need to call me and tell me where you are. I made dinner and now it's cold." There were tears in her eyes.

A "sorry" was on the tip of his tongue. He had to fight against it.

"I said I was going to Binny's after school, Mom," he said. "I told you last night, and you said that was cool and that there was no hurry to get home."

She dabbed her eyes with a tissue. Lionel put his backpack down by the sofa and sat at the table. She was really crying now. This was dumb. He decided to get it over with.

"I'm sorry, Mom. I'll call next time. I was being stupid as usual and forgot. Sorry. You don't have to cry."

She shook her head violently and crumpled the tissue in her fist. "I'm doing it again, aren't I? And don't apologize to me," she said.

That made it three people who didn't want him to say sorry. Then why was she crying?

"I should explain," she said. "My ... counsellor told me I need to communicate better and to stop feeling sorry for myself and taking it out on other people. Her name's Andrea." She cleared her throat and looked up with half-closed eyes. "I'm starting in the middle of the story, aren't I? Anyway, Sheila came to talk to me earlier this week, and she said I needed to speak to someone from Human Resources — they deal with employees whenever there's a problem. I knew right then and there I was being fired. It made sense since I thought Sheila hated me so much. I went without a word. Figured I should get it over with. I had some nasty thoughts, though. And guess what?"

Lionel's chin sunk to his chest. Fired! She complained and complained and complained about her job, but she always said it would be impossible to find a job like that again with a big company that paid well. His mom had said tons of times that the pension alone made it worth staying, even though she hated Sheila. He felt his stomach begin to tighten.

"I have eighty dollars from working at the café, and maybe I can find part-time work," he said.

She was laughing.

"How is this funny, Mom?"

What if she didn't find a new job?

"Lionel, I wasn't fired." She wiped her eyes. "Far from it. The HR woman, Andrea, is a counsellor for people to talk to, about life, and their problems, and how they feel, and stuff like that. Sheila just wanted me to talk to her — to help me. It was real weird at first, talking to a stranger about myself. Even weirder was that once I started I couldn't stop, must've talked for five hours — honest — and Andrea just listened. Sheila didn't even get angry when I came back. I even got paid for the time with Andrea! I told Sheila I'd use up my holidays, but she told me it was okay. I've met with Andrea every day this week for an hour to two, mostly over lunch or at breaks or after work." She patted his hand. "I'm embarrassing you, aren't I?"

He shook his head, even though she was.

She wasn't fooled. "Kids don't like hearing about their parents' problems. I've been loading mine onto you, and everyone else, for too long, and I feel bad about it. And I feel bad about how I've treated Sheila. We've talked a little this week and she's actually nice. I've always looked at things from my perspective and never hers. All she wanted was for me to do my job and be a team player, and all I wanted was to be a victim and get people to feel sorry for me." A tear fell. "Mostly, I feel guilty about how I've treated you, complaining and whining and being negative. Andrea's been telling me to stop blaming others for my problems and to do something with my life if I'm not happy, and that got me thinking of you, and how you cleaned up your room, and how you're running and getting in shape, and you're earning some money even, and how you got me to start cooking and not ordering in fast food all the time, which is another thing I feel guilty about. And, well, I want to tell you how proud I am of you and what you've been doing, and that I love you like crazy, and that, well, I went ahead and did something crazy myself."

Lionel blinked several times. That was most definitely his

mom sitting in front of him, but it didn't sound like her. She was talking fast and waving her hands in the air, and she had this weird energy.

"And when you walked in ... well ... I was upset with myself, not you. I wanted you home early so we could eat together. I made chicken with brown rice and salad. I got the recipe from the internet, this site called the Runner's Diet, which has all these tips and recipes for runners. I got so caught up in the cooking, I forgot you told me about working at the café — and now I gotta go!" She went to the counter and put a plate of food in front of him.

The Runner's Diet?

"Let me explain," she said, grabbing her purse. "When I met your father I was actually taking a bookkeeping course, which is learning how to keep track of money for businesses. I quit the course when I got pregnant with you ... and ... this is the crazy part ... I registered for another bookkeeping course and the first class is tonight, so I gotta go or I'll be late. Sorry. I wanted to have dinner with you and explain the Runner's Diet."

"We can do that later, Mom."

"You're so sweet. Thanks. I might be a bit late, so maybe tomorrow."

That sounded kinda funny, like she was asking permission, like she was the kid and he was the parent, and he began to laugh, and so did she.

The idea of his mom going back to school was a bit insane, but she seemed so excited about it, so happy, so into it, he wasn't gonna be the one to say she shouldn't. In a way, she sounded like him when he began running. Maybe she'd love bookkeeping the way he loved to run.

"I think it's a great idea, Mom ... if that's what you want to do."

"Thanks, Li." She gave him a kiss, then leaned her head back. "Where did you get that watch?" she said.

"Oh ... you know Donna?"

"The nice lady down the hall? She's a real character. Talks my ear off."

"Yeah, her. Well ... she found out I was jogging a bit and ... she bought me this watch. It's a smart watch."

It struck him how ridiculous it was for him to wear it. He liked saying it, though.

He also liked that his mom was doing stuff, like him and the running. Maybe she would like it and ... be happier.

It then struck him that they were a family too, he and his mom, every bit as much as Kiana's.

## Saturday: 9:00 a.m.

Deepak swung his arms in wild circles. "So, I was figuring we run to the ravine and back and laugh at Afonso when he passes out. He'll want us to call an ambulance, but I say we don't because it'll slow us down. Worst case scenario, he dies. I'm willing to take the risk."

"I'm going to pass out from the color of your shorts," Afonso said.

Deepak began to jog on the spot. "Yellow is an energy color. You'd best get used to seeing these way out in front."

Afonso grunted. "No chance I'm running behind those banana pants. Get used to the back of my shirt."

Deepak rubbed his chin with his fingers. "You might have a point. Last time I ran more than twenty yards was … Can't actually remember." His face grew troubled. "I'm out of shape. All I do is go to school, work at the store, and go to piano lessons. I'm like an old man." He pulled his shoulders back. "This is going to be painful, but I need it. Will you guys promise to carry me back when I collapse into the fetal position and start sucking my thumb?"

"We'll drag you back by your heels — or those shorts," Afonso said.

"I knew I could count on you," Deepak gushed.

Lionel didn't know where to look or how to stand or even how to hold his arms. He could never joke around. Nick and his buds were always giving each other a hard time — and the meaner the insult, the harder they laughed. Deepak and Afonso were a little different. Their disses were funny — but not bully-mean like Nick's vicious put-downs.

"Where are Kiana and Georgina?" Deepak said.

Kiana had sent a text yesterday to meet at the café at nine o'clock.

"There's Georgina," Deepak said. He waved his hand over his head. "At least run it in. You're a Marketeer now."

She jogged over, her head down. "I can't believe we're actually doing this," she said.

Georgina didn't look like she was running anywhere. She wore her big black boots and had long black socks that went to the middle of her thighs, with a short black skirt, and a black T-shirt with a black fishnet shirt on top.

"I can't believe Afonso is doing this either," Deepak said.

"He'll do great," Georgina said.

Afonso bowed his head slightly.

Kiana came out of the café. "Awesome, we're all here. Had to deal with the parents. Apparently, I stayed out too late last night. Anyway … this is such a great idea. I'm so stoked. I tried to set up a running club at school and no one ever showed up."

Kiana glanced at Georgina. "I thought you had this morning off so you could run with us," she said.

Georgina's eyes hardened. "I am …"

"You're running in that?" Kiana said.

"What do you want me to run in?" Georgina said.

Kiana suddenly laughed and she patted Georgina's shoulder. "You're the best, George. I love it. I should be more like you and wear what I want. I'm such a fashion victim."

Georgina bit her lower lip and smiled, her eyelashes flickering. "Don't know about that," she murmured.

Kiana wore blue tights with a black stripe up the sides and a pink and blue top. Lionel thought she looked ... athletic.

"So are we the Marketeers Running Club or the Marketeers Stand Around and Do Nothing Club?" Kiana said.

"I vote for the second one," Deepak said.

"You would," Kiana said.

"So where should we go? The ravine?" Afonso said.

They all looked at each other.

"The ravine it is," Kiana said.

The door opened and Binny came out. "Good. Got you before you left." He tugged on the leash and Britney popped out the door. Britney sniffed the air and went over to Kiana. She bent and patted her head and rubbed her belly.

"This young lady needs a good run," Binny said. "I want her back five pounds lighter."

"We'd have to run for a couple days for that, Daddy," Kiana said.

Binny handed her the leash. "Do what it takes. Good luck to you and don't forget to come back for some smoothies. Runners need to keep up their protein."

"Smoothie's don't have protein," Kiana said.

Binny flicked his eyebrows. "They do when I make them."

"Yum," Deepak said. "Bacon smoothies."

Kiana wrapped the end of the leash around her hand. "Marketeers away," she declared.

She and Britney set off down the street. Georgina fell in behind, and then Deepak and Afonso. Lionel brought up the rear, which suited him fine. They wouldn't see his bouncing stomach. He had a feeling Deepak would make a joke about it. They continued along for a few blocks, very slowly. Lionel had to force himself to drop back. This was slow even for him. He figured they were just warming up.

"Please tell me we're at the ravine," Deepak said.

"We're at the ravine," Afonso said.

"Really?"

"No."

Deepak groaned. Lionel laughed to himself. Those two were funny. They continued for a few more blocks — and then it hit him. They were running slowly for him. Don't leave the fat slob behind. Maybe that was nice, in a weird way, but it bugged him, too. He and Britney went way faster than this. Britney was actually a pretty good runner for a small, chubby dog. Those little legs could motor.

"Whoa, Mister Flash," Deepak said.

Lionel blew past them. Kiana and Georgina were fifteen yards ahead. They stopped suddenly, and he slowed to see what was up.

"C'mon, Britney," Kiana said. "Don't be like that."

"She doesn't want to run?" Lionel said. "Is she faking it?"

Britney scratched behind her ears with her back paw.

"Not sure," Kiana said. "Are you being a bad doggie?"

"She hasn't pretended to hurt herself for a while," Lionel said. He knelt down and patted her. "What's wrong, Brit? You can run way longer than this."

Britney put her two front paws on his thighs and licked his cheek.

"Whoever decided to rest is my hero and I will worship them forever," Deepak said, breathing heavily.

Kiana put the leash in Lionel's hand.

"You run with her," Kiana said. "I think she wants you."

Lionel stood up. "She likes you best. She won't run with me if she won't with you."

"I'm liking our recess, by the way," Deepak said, his chest heaving.

Deepak should stop pretending he was tired and just run, Lionel thought. Sometimes he pushed a joke too far.

"Are we gonna take a break every five minutes?" Afonso said.

"You're getting on my nerves," Deepak said to him.

Afonso grinned. "C'mon Lionel. Take the lead and let's go. I've got a soccer season to get ready for. I was thinking about this last night. I'm always too tired during a game to do much, especially in the second half. I want to be a good player."

"And I have the city finals to make," Kiana said.

"I think I need to get a pair of running shoes," Georgina said. "Not sure what I was thinking with these clodhoppers."

"Come over to the store after the run and I'll find you a pair," Deepak said. "We have tons of shoes in the back that won't cost much. Not sure the color …"

"It doesn't matter," Georgina said quickly.

Lionel took the leash and gave it a tug. Britney bounced to her feet. She let out a few barks and began to run. Lionel had no choice but to go too. The others fell in behind. Britney wouldn't slow down, however, and she began to strain against the leash. Lionel had to run faster so she wouldn't choke herself. He caught a couple of green lights and still she kept at it. He sensed someone running on his right and he moved over.

"I can't believe that's my Britney," Kiana said.

"She can go pretty fast when she wants to," Lionel said. He looked over his shoulder. Deepak and Afonso were way back. Georgina was about twenty yards behind.

"That's because Britney's such a good doggie, isn't she?" Kiana said. "You're such a Britney and you love running like your master. Right? That's why."

Kiana ran so easily, so effortlessly, so gracefully, as if her feet barely touched the sidewalk. Stride for stride she matched him, with Britney's feet scurrying like mad, as they crossed another intersection and continued up the street. He enjoyed being with Kiana — until he began to feel the pressure of conversation. They couldn't run next to each other and not say a word. He didn't dare talk about school, that was a minefield, and she didn't strike him as a gamer. No chance he'd tell her about his running chart. She'd think that was geeky. Britney barked and pulled on the leash. That gave him an idea. She loved Britney.

"She's into it now," he said.

"Let's see what she can do, then," Kiana said. She ran faster. Lionel kept up. Britney barked a few times, her feet moving so fast it was a blur of paws. He'd never seen Britney look so happy. She kept letting out a bark every few yards and her tail was wagging insanely. Lionel began to worry that Kiana would notice the sweat dripping down his forehead. He was overheating in his sweatshirt and sweatpants.

Kiana looked down at Britney and then smiled at him. She sure loved that dog, Lionel thought. He'd stick with that.

"Is she yours? Is she your dog, I mean?" he said.

"Dad bought her for my birthday, so I guess she is," Kiana said.

"I've never had a dog," Lionel said. "My mom says it's not fair to leave a dog in an apartment all day. She works at a grocery store and I'm at school."

"Is there anyone else ... at home?"

"My dad and mom split up a few years ago."

He'd leave Brent out of it.

"Do you see your dad much?"

"Not really. He moved to another town and he's busy. Got married again. He has a couple of kids now — boys, I think."

"So you have two brothers — or half-brothers."

"I guess."

"I take it you guys aren't that close."

"Not really."

"That's too bad."

Sometimes he wondered what those kids were like, his half-brothers, and what his dad did with them. He probably took them to baseball and played with them in the park and stuff. Truth was, he'd never met his half-brothers, and as for his dad, he hadn't laid eyes on him since the night he left six years ago.

They continued on. The Britney topic was used up. What else could they talk about? The ravine was only about two hundred yards away and the silence was gruelling. She must think he was the most boring kid in the world.

"Sorry for asking about your dad," Kiana said finally. "It must've been a hard thing to go through."

"I guess."

She looked over, as if expecting him to say more.

"I don't think much about it, to be honest," he said. "I mean, he left, his choice. Nothing I can do about it. If he doesn't want to see me ..."

"How often do you see him, then?"

"Not too often — basically, never."

The sound of their feet, the clicking of Britney's nails, created a rhythm of sorts, a soft, comforting sound. The ravine was up ahead. He wondered what it would be like to keep going, with her, until he couldn't go any further.

## Saturday: 9:21 a.m.

Kiana and Lionel stopped at the top of the hill where the path led down to the ravine. People passed on the sidewalk.

"Let's wait on the grass," Kiana said.

He followed her down the hill a bit. Somehow they'd gotten

way ahead. He figured the others must've hit some red lights. Kiana sat down and stretched her legs out. They were long and strong-looking, but still slender. He forced himself not to look. He sat down far enough away that she wouldn't be grossed out by his sweat.

"You're dressed like it's the middle of January," she said, with a laugh. "I'd be melting if I wore that."

She had no idea. He shrugged and looked away.

"Hmm. Okay, let's not talk fashion." She sat up, her face bright, and looked keenly at him. "On Monday, are you going to read your story?"

She needed to stop with that. He never should've told her.

"Maybe."

"It's a great-sounding story. Just read it or Whellan's going to give you a zero."

"Okay. Maybe," he said.

"You were going to send it to me," she said. "I'll read it tonight if you want."

"I ... uh ... Maybe if I get it done."

Georgina ran across the street, puffing fairly hard. "My feet are killing me," she said. "I'm such an idiot."

"You should get a pair like Lionel," Kiana said.

"I love them," Georgina said. "Where'd you get them?"

"At Deepak's ... I mean, at his dad's store," Lionel said.

"The Green Machine," Kiana declared. "He's a born runner."

"Do they have jet packs in them?" Georgina said. "I knew Kiana could run, but I can't believe how fast you are."

Lionel allowed himself a smile.

"I wonder if they come in black," Georgina said.

The boys staggered over. Afonso put his hands on his knees. He was breathing heavily. Deepak threw himself on the grass.

"Can't breathe. Can't move. Leave me here to die," Deepak said.

"You're doing okay," Georgina said.

"You'll make it," Kiana said.

"You're insane," Deepak said.

"I say we kick Deepak outta the Marketeers for excessive whining," Afonso said.

Lionel shot Kiana a concerned look.

"He's kidding," Kiana whispered.

Deepak raised his head and then let it flop back. "I say Kiana and Lionel carry me."

"I want in on that being carried thing," Afonso said.

"You guys are doing great," Kiana said. "I've been training for two months already, and Lionel runs all the time."

That lie was officially out of control.

"We should get going," Kiana said, getting up. "We shouldn't let ourselves cool down — muscles will get tight."

"Fine," Deepak grumbled. He stuffed his phone in his pocket. "Help me up at least."

He held out his hand. Afonso took it and pulled. Deepak's shoulders lifted off the ground — and then collapsed back.

Kiana and Georgina took his other hand, and all three of them heaved on the count of three.

Deepak beat his chest weakly with his fists and let out a pathetic Tarzan call. He rolled his neck and did a deep knee bend. "Ready to run back or die trying."

"That should be the Marketeers' battle cry," Afonso said. "Run or Death."

"That's maybe not as inspiring as the Musketeers' 'All for one and one for all,'" Kiana said, "but it gets the job done." She looked at Lionel. "I brought my copy of *The Three Musketeers*. Remind me to give it to you."

"Great. Thanks," Lionel croaked.

Now he was going to have to read it.

"Run or Death," Deepak cried, and he started off.

"I knew it would catch on," Afonso said. He ran across the street after him.

Georgina hopped up on her toes. "See ya back at the café." She took a few steps and then turned back. "You should carry me. I'm the lightest."

"I'll let Lionel do it. He could carry all four of us and still win," Kiana said.

Lionel wondered why she'd say a ridiculous thing like that. Made no sense.

"Run or Death!" Georgina said, thrusting her right fist over her head.

Georgina was different somehow during this run, more relaxed. She looked like a little kitten, a black kitten naturally, but a cute one. She was a nice-looking girl, not like Kiana, but still nice.

"C'mon, Lionel," Kiana said. "You in the mood to hoof it? I'm feeling stoked and Britney's on fire."

"I guess."

"Green light means go," Kiana said, digging her elbow into his ribs. She raced across the intersection.

Lionel gave Britney's leash a tug. It didn't take long to catch Kiana. Britney was on fire. All she seemed to want to do was run. They ran past Kiana.

"I knew you were gonna cheat," Kiana said.

"Your dog's gone mad," he said over his shoulder.

Next they tore past Georgina.

"I want those shoes," Georgina called out.

As usual, he couldn't think of a joke. Deepak and Afonso were next.

"Boo!" Afonso jeered, as he passed them. "Big show off."

"I'd run fast too — if I wasn't slow," Deepak said.

It didn't sound like chirping — and he was an expert on that.

Sounded more like they were trying to be funny. He wanted to say something funny back, but as usual, nothing came to mind.

So he kept running.

The lights were cooperating and he kept hitting the greens. He turned the final corner and cruised to Binny's.

"You did great, Brit," he said, petting her back.

Britney's sides were heaving and her tongue hung out of her mouth.

"I think you're getting skinnier," he said. "Maybe you haven't lost five pounds, but you will if you keep this up."

Truth was, Lionel was losing weight too. Hard to know for sure, but he'd had to tighten his belt a couple notches for his jeans, and his stomach felt less jiggly, at least a little. Probably all in his head.

He looked up the street and almost did a double-take. Kiana was still half a block back. How dumb was he? He'd had a chance to run with her and maybe talk about something. Instead, Mister Fat and Stupid gallops off like a racehorse. He tried to think of something clever to say.

"When did you learn to run like that?" she said, breathlessly.

"I wasn't that fast," he said.

"Wrong, you are very fast," she said.

"Not really — I got lucky — hit some green lights," he said.

She crossed her arms. "Accept it, Lionel. You're fast," she said in an even tone.

Lionel looked down at the pavement and pretended he needed to stretch so he wouldn't look like a goof.

Kiana opened the café door. "I'm looking forward to hearing your story on Monday," she said.

The door closed before he could answer.

## Monday: 9:45 a.m.

*Abidemi felt a sting in his leg and then his back. He staggered a few more steps — and fell face first to the hard, dry ground. He couldn't move.*

*Rat-a tat-tat.*

*The machine guns kept firing, relentlessly.*

*"Abidemi, get up. We're almost there. The border is just over that hill."*

*He raised his head. His legs were dead. "I'm hit, Gebburza. I can't. You have to take care of them. Go."*

*The crackle of gunfire whistled overhead. Abidemi saw the others running. A few border guards provided cover by firing back at the rebels.*

*"You have to go," Abidemi said, pushing her away. "You'll get caught. They need you."*

*"I'm not leaving you. We're so close."*

*He smiled and gripped her hand. "This is how it has to be. Go," he said firmly.*

*He was worried his strength would fail him before he convinced her to get across the border — to safety.*

*Gebbuza wiped the tears from her eyes. Abidemi knew she could do it. She was tough — as tough as any of them. Gebbuza squeezed his hand, and then ran off without looking back.*

*He was able to watch her until she disappeared over the hill, then his head fell back. The pain was gone, but now he was cold, terribly cold, even though the sun burned brightly in the sky.*

*The gunfire stopped.*

*He smiled to himself. They'd crossed a desert, waded a raging river, fought off wild animals, hid from rebels — and now they were free. A bunch of kids, and they'd done it. Abidemi cast a last, wistful look to the sky. So close. Better to remember Gebbuza's face, her eyes, her voice.*

*The light faded.*

*"This one's dead," the rebel said. "Do you want his clothes?" He kicked Abidemi's lifeless body.*

*"What are we going to do with those rags? The hyenas will take care of the body," the commander said. "Back to the base. Move out."*

*The commander walked away, and the others followed close behind. The rebel who kicked Abidemi waited until they'd gone ahead. He turned and bent down.*

*"Goodbye, little brother," he said. "At least you don't have to fight anymore. Say hello to Mother and Father in heaven. I know I will never see them again."*

*He wiped away a tear, cast a longing look at the border, and followed his unit back into the jungle.*

Lionel lowered his papers to the desk. His palms were hot and damp. A drop of sweat dripped down the back of his neck. He was so light-headed, he wondered if he was getting sick again. The class was dead quiet. Whellan had a surprised look on his face.

Lionel had done it — read his story in class. He'd done it for Kiana. He couldn't stand the thought of disappointing her. He couldn't.

"I am ... Wow ... I'm kinda at a loss for words," Whellan said. "To be honest, I wasn't expecting anything like that. I loved it. Your story has all the elements we've been speaking about: character development, plot, climax, pathos. It had moments of humor, of drama, tragedy. You've obviously done a lot of work to learn so much about the civil war in the Congo." He looked around the class. "Comments?"

Lionel gripped the edges of his papers. Stephane's hand went up. Lionel closed his eyes. "Please don't," he thought. "Please don't make me like you."

"I felt like I was there, with those kids, as they went from village to village, hiding from soldiers and looking for a way to cross the border to safety," Stephane gushed. "I was on the edge of my seat a few times wondering if they'd make it. It's sad that the leader, Abidemi, died. I wanted him to survive. But maybe it would've been unrealistic if everyone made it."

"I saw a documentary on Africa, recently," Angelina said. "It was about child soldiers and how kids are forced to fight, and they make them take drugs and beat them if they don't do what they're told. Lionel's story reminded me of that, how unfair the world can be, especially to kids."

"I liked the part at the end, when they ran for the border and the guns were firing at them," Jaime said.

The bell rang.

Whellan tossed his hands in the air. "Typical. Just when an interesting discussion starts, we have to leave. That's school for you. Unfortunately, we have to deal with more grammar Thursday because we have a test coming up." Nick and Bryan booed and Whellan bowed his head. "Sorry, but that's another reality of school. Remind me and we can pick this discussion up next week because it's an important topic involving kids your age, and obviously there are people here knowledgeable about it. Good work, Lionel. It was worth the wait. Now I gotta scoot to a staff meeting, so I apologize for the hasty departure. See you in three days." Whellan nodded to the class, scooped up his satchel, and left.

Lionel's ears and neck tingled. Saved by the bell. The kids were going to come at him now. A quick getaway was the only play. He needed to disappear, and no way he was coming to class Thursday. He needed to get the flu real quick — and for a week. Dumbest thing he'd ever done: try to impress a girl he barely knew, who put up with him because they ran together a few times a week. He got up.

"Hey, Congo Man, you get those choice shoes from Africa?" Nick said.

"I didn't notice those beauties," Bryan said. "Were they the last pair of shoes in the world and you had to buy them?"

Stephane snuck past and shot him a sympathetic look. A few other kids kept their eyes firmly on the floor as they left. Lionel didn't blame them. He would've done the same — in a heartbeat. They were doing the smart thing.

"In my opinion, Mr. Whellan," Nick said, in a high-pitched voice, "it's too bad those kids didn't get wasted right away so we didn't have to suffer through that lame story."

"Or look at those shoes," Bryan said.

"Maybe you'd run as fast as Lionel if you had shoes like that," Kiana said to Bryan.

Bryan reacted as if he'd seen aliens land on Earth. "I run the fifteen hundred on the freakin' track team, Kiana. Are they magic shoes or something?"

"They must be covered in pixie dust," Nick said. "That's the only way you get that color."

"Lionel would beat you by a hundred yards easy," Kiana shot back.

"Maybe in an eating competition," Nick said.

"You're so rude," Kiana said.

She looked over at Lionel. Her eyes blazed with fury. He stared back helplessly, and slowly her eyes grew soft and her anger melted away. In its place he saw something much worse: disappointment.

"Sorry, Kiana," Nick said. "But you gotta admit, those shoes are disturbing."

He and Bryan burst out laughing.

Lionel stepped out from behind his desk. The door was fifteen feet away. Fifteen feet and he was gone, and this was over, at least for now; maybe if he got lucky it would be over for good. He could miss a week of classes, with the flu or headaches or anything, and they'd forget about him. And somehow he had to get new shoes.

Rashmi pulled on Kiana's arm. "Let's go," she said.

Kiana's face was pale. She seemed close to tears. The sight wrenched his heart.

"I'm in," Lionel said.

Bryan's eyes screwed up tightly and he took a step towards him. "You're in for what?" he said.

"For the race. Let's do it," Lionel said. His voice shook slightly.

Bryan's eyes bugged out and a half-smile spread across his face. "Bro, didn't you hear I'm on the track team and you're ..."

"Like a big fat sponge," Nick finished for him.

Words tumbled out before Lionel could stop himself. "You wanna see how these shoes work, then step up. I got you figured as the hot-air type, but who knows?"

"You've lost it, Congo Man," Nick said.

"If you knew anything about running you'd know these are practically the best shoes money can buy," Lionel said. "By the way, Bryan, I heard no one else actually tried out for the fifteen hundred, so that's how you made the team."

Kiana had told him that.

Kiana giggled. The color had returned to her face, and he even saw a hint of a smile.

"Done, bro," Bryan said, snatching his books. "We'll go twice around the track."

"And the loser's gotta jog one more lap in his underwear," Nick said.

He held up his hand and Bryan gave him a tentative high-five.

"You always have to do that," Kiana said to Nick.

"Do what?" he said.

"Push it — and try to embarrass people," she said.

"What's the big deal, Kiana? It's just a race — with a kicker at the end," Nick laughed.

"Fine," she snapped. "But if Bryan loses, you gotta do it too."

"And you?" Nick said.

She held out her hand.

Nick grinned and shook it. "This is a bad idea, girlfriend, not that I would mind seeing you in your undies."

"I'm not your girlfriend," Kiana said.

"Whoa, I'm just joking around," Nick said.

"I'm not," Kiana said.

"This is dumb," Rashmi said to Kiana. "Don't do this."

"I ain't worried," Kiana said, "and it's a bet."

"Okay, Kiana, what color panties you wearing?" Nick said. He held up his cellphone "I wanna make sure I get a good pic."

He and Bryan broke up again.

Kiana snorted in disgust.

"Make it three laps," Bryan said, "if you can handle it."

"Why not make it a real fifteen hundred?" Nick said.

Bryan held out his hand. Lionel shook it. Bryan's hand was cool and dry.

Bryan let go and waved his hand in the air. "Gross, bro. Sweat much?"

"Meet at the track after school," Nick said.

"No way he shows," Bryan said.

He and Nick left.

"Kiana, what's gotten into you?" Rashmi said.

Kiana tossed her head back and shrugged. "I'm not worried, so you shouldn't be." She looked into Lionel's eyes. "Accept it, Lionel. You're fast," she said, cuffing Rashmi's arm.

They left. He was alone.

That's what she'd said at the end of their run. It hadn't made much sense then, and it made less sense now. Nick was right. He was a big, fat sponge. But there was no backing out now. He was all in. He'd never survive school if he lost this race, and Kiana would never forgive him, not ever, for real this time. If she had to run around the track in her underwear and bra ...

He blanked out for a bit, the dizziness returning.

*Accept it, Lionel. You're fast.*

He wanted to be fast.

But he wasn't.

## Monday: 3:45 p.m.

Bryan kicked at a few pebbles on the track and pointed to a white pole. "Listen up, Green Shoes. It's three times around, and the fourth lap ends at the white pole. You gotta beat me by a hundred feet or I win."

"That's not the bet," Lionel flashed.

"Your girlfriend said you could," Bryan grinned. "You heard her, and you and me shook on it."

"That wasn't what we said," Lionel stammered.

"So you admit she's your girlfriend," Bryan snickered.

"I didn't say that," Lionel said.

"She's not his girlfriend," Nick said.

"Doesn't matter," Kiana said. "Lionel will win by two hundred feet."

Nick laughed. "I love your sense of humor," he said to Kiana. "Anyway, let's get this done." He walked about ten yards ahead and held up an arm. "On the count of three, gentlemen."

"Bury this guy," Kiana said.

Lionel put his toe behind the white line. He noticed a group of kids looking their way, including Stephane, Jaime, and Angelina. He had a feeling they weren't there by accident. Word had spread. Nick or Bryan had probably posted about the race online. He looked around. There were lots of small groups gathered about.

"Ready!" Nick said.

Bryan stepped forward, left knee and arm bent, chest forward, both hands clenched.

That stupid story. Whellan didn't care. Kiana didn't care. He could've gotten a zero and it would've been done.

Kiana will hate him forever and the Marketeers will be over too.

"Get set. Go!"

Nick threw his arm down. Bryan took off like a sprinter, his arms chugging furiously. Lionel gave chase and caught up quickly, trying to stay close until he got a feel for the track. He'd never run a race on a track before, and the track looked huge.

Fifteen hundred meters! This was nuts.

"Try out this heat," Bryan said, and he pushed the pace.

Lionel was almost glad to run faster. It kept his mind off what was at stake. He decided to match Bryan's stride as a way of settling his nerves, and they continued around the second curve and into the front straightaway. Lionel was finding the pace a little slow, so he shifted outside and pulled up even. Bryan gasped, his breathing labored like an old-fashioned train huffing and puffing up a hill. He looked over and Lionel almost gasped himself. The strained look on Bryan's face, the tightly drawn mouth, the pale face — Bryan was scared.

And Lionel was an expert on scared.

Then it hit him. Bryan couldn't keep up; he'd gone out too fast — he was done. Lionel could win, actually win. It was a strange thought — winning. He'd never won anything in his life, unless you count video games, and that wasn't really winning. He was going to win a race, at school, in front of all these people, in front of Kiana, and Nick, and Jaime, and Angelina ... the entire school would know. A surge of energy flooded his body, from head to toe: an electric charge.

Kiana was right.

He was fast.

Lionel began to separate himself from Bryan, first a half-yard, then a full one. He could see Kiana up ahead pumping her fists.

"Bryan! Move your freakin' butt," Nick screamed.

Lionel felt something clip his back heel.

His arms flailed over his head and his feet lifted off the ground. He fluttered through the air like an out-of-control bird — until his chest and forearms hit the track.

The first thing he heard was Nick cheering. Lionel looked up. Bryan hadn't broken stride. He was at least thirty feet up the track, almost at the white pole. Kiana looked horrified, hands cupping her face. He could only imagine what she was thinking: what a klutz, what a loser, what a pathetic loser. Bryan had tripped him, but he'd done it from behind. No one had seen it. Lionel forced himself to get up and hobble a step. His right knee throbbed. Blood was oozing from the side. A small stone had lodged itself under the skin. He pressed against it and the stone popped out. More blood dipped down his leg.

This wasn't fair.

This was the most unfair thing that had ever happened.

He would've won: he knew it.

This was more unfair than his dad leaving, more unfair than getting yelled at for striking out, more unfair than having to live in a small, smelly apartment, more unfair than the bus pulling away, more unfair than all the bullying he'd put up with in his entire life.

Anger welled up — and it disappeared the next instant.

Bryan had only done what any scared kid would do.

And then the truth hit him.

It hit him harder than anything he'd ever felt — harder than hitting the ground, harder than any spanking from his dad.

He'd let himself fall. He'd gone down way too easily. He'd dropped like a sack of potatoes — a Do-Nothing. A horrible tightness in his chest, a bitter taste in his mouth, a tingle at the back of his neck that trickled down his spine, a dull thud in his head — his old friends all came back.

He began to run.

No anger, no shame, no worry, no fear, he just ran as fast and hard as he could. He could see Nick yelling at him, but he didn't hear a word. Kiana looked more ghost than real. He didn't notice the onlookers. He didn't see Bryan ahead of him. His mind was empty. All that remained was the track, the sound of his shoes, and his breath.

Nothing to slow him down.

By the back straight, he'd caught up. He moved a good two feet to the side and blasted past Bryan as if he was standing still, a statue in the way, a pylon, nothing. Lionel felt anger at that moment, and for the first time in his life he understood how angry he really was, and how that had made him into a Do-Nothing. He'd been angry at a world that didn't care, so angry that he'd made himself invisible — and still the world didn't care. Anger wasn't the answer. Being invisible didn't make the pain go away.

He wasn't invisible now. They saw him — him — on this track, running, doing something.

He came into the front straightaway and pumped his arms and raised his knees, urging himself to go faster and faster. There was no slowing down now — not ever again.

"You're ahead by at least twenty yards," Kiana shrieked excitedly as he went by. She was clapping and jumping up and down.

"Run, you idiot," Nick yelled at Bryan. "Aren't you on the stupid track team? You're losing to the biggest doofus in school!"

Lionel chewed the ground up, yard by yard, the corner, the back straightaway, the second corner. Kiana was cheering him on. The kids watching were clapping in unison.

"Faster," he said to himself. "Faster. You can go faster."

Do something for once in your life.

Kiana jumped out in front of him and held up her hands. "What color undies you got on, Nicky?" she said.

Lionel moved over. What was she doing?

"Hold up, Lionel. Race is over. He's walking," Kiana said.

Lionel looked over his shoulder. Bryan had quit rounding the second corner and was cutting across the infield, his hands on his hips, head down. He seemed to be limping.

Nick and Bryan were going to kill him, of course. School was about to become a nightmare. He would take over from Stephane as the school punching bag.

But this was worth it.

"Yeah, Lionel. Yeah, Lionel. Yeaaahhhh, Lionel," Kiana sang, imitating a cheerleader, kicking her heels up and holding a fist over her head.

He let himself smile.

"You're such a loser," Nick said to Bryan. "I knew I should've run instead of you. Seriously. You run like a beached whale — that has asthma."

"I pulled a muscle ... like when we started," Bryan said. "I told you I was tight and needed to warm up. I can never run good without warming up."

Lionel had so wanted to enjoy this, to see Bryan and Nick humiliated in front of everyone — like those stupid stories in Whellan's class when the bully finally got bullied.

But all he felt was sadness.

"Let's forget the bet," Lionel said. "I wasn't serious. Stupid thing to bet on."

Bryan stared, open-mouthed.

"What?" Rashmi said. "They lost, and they would've made you do it, trust me."

"I wasn't going to make Kiana run in her underwear," Nick said. "I was joking. C'mon, Rashmi. You know me."

Rashmi gave Nick a stern look.

"It's dumb," Lionel said. "It was just a race. I'm going home. So ... let's forget it."

Rashmi half-laughed and looked over at Kiana.

"That's fair, I guess," Nick said, "since he pulled a muscle. If someone got hurt ... and it's not like I was going to make you do it, Kiana."

Kiana stared hard at Nick, and then shrugged. "If Lionel doesn't care, I don't. I've gotta go, too."

"Hey, Kiana. Let's just go to Pearl's. On me. We were joking about the underwear," Nick said. "No big deal. C'mon. Rashmi, what do you say?"

"I'm gonna go home," Kiana said.

"I should go too ... lots of homework," Rashmi said.

Kiana pointed at Bryan. "Go buy yourselves some real shoes,

cowboy," she said.

Rashmi let out a short laugh. "I'll talk to you later, Kia. See you, boys. Good running, Lionel. Never knew you had it in you."

Rashmi began to walk towards the school. Lionel felt awkward, standing there with Kiana, Nick, and Bryan, knowing the other kids were watching.

He decided to leave … after he said one more thing!

"You two don't have to be such jerks … to guys like Stephane," he said. "You could leave him alone. It's so stupid. If you don't like someone, don't talk to them. Guys like you … think you're special … you think …" He paused to catch his breath. "If you asked around you'd be surprised what people really think of you."

Nick looked at Lionel blankly. He puffed out his cheeks, and then with a slight shrug, offered a grin. Bryan stood still, head down.

"I'll see you later," Lionel said to Kiana. He picked up his backpack and headed to the field.

"Wait up," Kiana called.

Lionel kept walking. He was finished: no words, no feelings, other than a need to get away, to leave this behind. Tomorrow was a long way off. He'd go for a run tonight, the longest of his life, and he wasn't going to worry about tomorrow. Sure, it would come: the chirping, the bullying, the humiliation. He wasn't taking these shoes off, though. Not ever.

A hand grabbed his shoulder. "Hey, Lionel. Didn't you hear me?" Kiana asked.

She sounded like her feelings were hurt.

His chest got tight. What was it about this girl that mixed him up so much?

"Sorry. Yeah, I heard, but I was … I don't know what I was, to be honest. Messed up about that dumb race."

She flicked her eyebrows. "You sure did win that dumb race, though."

"I guess I did."

They continued toward the gate at the top of the hill.

"I can't believe how you smoked him after you fell," Kiana said. "I've never seen anyone run like that. You were ... I don't know ... Amazing."

"I guess I got pretty mad. I think he tripped me."

"I knew it," Kiana said, slapping her hands together. "He's such a snake. Tripping a guy — I bet he faked being hurt."

She sounded furious. Weird. He wasn't actually that angry about it — more mad at himself.

"It's over. Doesn't matter. I don't blame him. He wanted to win."

"You're too nice. It's cheating and ..." She laughed, and suddenly didn't seem that angry either. "I'm being silly. You're right. You smoked him and everyone knows it."

"I guess."

"Hmm. You don't seem too excited about it."

Truth was he didn't know what to think. His head was in a whirl. He still couldn't believe what had happened. "Not sure I should be excited. Things will be interesting for me tomorrow."

She jumped in front of him and held out her arm. "Those boys try anything, you tell me."

"What are you going to do?"

She grinned and punched her palm with her fist. "I might have to break some heads or something."

He laughed at the way she said it, like a gangster.

Kiana moved aside and they began walking again. Suddenly, she whirled in front of him again and stuck her hand in his chest.

"I got it. Greatest idea ever." Her eyes were alive and she seemed possessed by this idea — like it actually was the greatest ever.

He looked at her and she looked back, grinning the entire time.

"Lionel, you're the most amazing person I've ever met."

He had no clue what she was going on about. She'd lost it.

"I say I have the greatest idea ever and you just wait for me to tell you."

"Um ... what's your idea?"

She laughed. "You're coming out for the track team."

So he could get picked on even more? "No thanks. I'm not really a team guy."

"It's track-and-field, not a team sport," she said. "You're an awesome runner. You are. I still can't believe how you ripped that last lap." She looked at him closely. "You never get tired, do you? Admit it."

"Of course I get tired."

"No, I mean when you're running. I've noticed, with the Marketeers, we're all puffing and you keep running, like you can't understand why we're going so slow."

Sometimes they did seem to go slow. He figured they were being nice to him.

Kiana put her hands on her hips and took a deep breath. "Will you promise me to at least think about it?"

"Not much to think about ..."

"Please? C'mon. You're such a good runner. Pick a distance event and go for it." She clapped her hands together. "Maybe the fifteen hundred? You have the speed and the stamina. I'm going to tell Whellan."

"No, don't," he said.

He said it louder than he meant to. The smile faded from Kiana's lips. She lifted her chin and let her shoulders relax.

"I don't actually have a boyfriend," she said.

His heart began pounding.

"Bryan is just chirping me," Lionel said. "Don't let him bug you."

"He doesn't bug me," Kiana said. "I just wanted you to know, to hear it from me. I wouldn't mind, having a boyfriend I mean, if it was the right boy. I don't have one now, is all. I've never had one, not really."

His throat had gone dry.

"You taking the bus to the Market?" she said.

He nodded.

"Wanna run back instead?" she said.

She took off. He followed her up the hill, and slowed at the top to let her go through the gate first.

## Thursday: 7:10 a.m.

Lionel stopped in front of the café. He'd felt strong this morning, wide awake the second his alarm went off. He'd run every day after school since his race with Bryan, and the Marketeers had run Tuesday and Wednesday too. Everyone was getting into it, even Deepak wasn't complaining.

Without running, Lionel would've lost his mind these past couple of days. Nick was all over him, or at least he tried to be. Lionel was pretty good at disappearing, in the library, in different parts of the school, in the park. Still, it had been pretty brutal. He could never relax, and had to be constantly on his guard. He could only hope Nick would let up soon. He didn't seem the *let up* type.

He didn't regret the race, though. He'd always remember it — and the look on Kiana's face. They'd gone to the café after and sat and talked for a couple of hours. Kiana teased him about a lot of things, like how quiet he was at school, and that he never hung out, and always went right home. He didn't care. It was fun to be with her, except when she asked about the track team; sometimes she'd be weird and just smile at him and her eyes would be so bright and alive it was hard not to stare. She even hugged him when they said goodbye.

He wiped his face with his T-shirt and looked down the street. Still no one. They must've stopped. Kiana and the others had teased him so much about running in his sweatshirt and

sweatpants that he finally ran this morning in shorts and a
t-shirt. He hated showing his flabby arms and legs and stomach,
although he had to admit it was way more comfortable. He
wasn't such a big sweat ball.

He was about to go inside the café to get his sweatshirt when
he spotted Kiana's bouncing hair about a half-block away. He
didn't want to be rude and look like he was taking off before
they even got back, as if he was some sort of big shot runner.
He waited, feeling a bit awkward. He folded his arms across his
chest, then let them fall, then crossed them again. He was such
a goof — didn't even know how to hold his arms.

"Hey, Speedy, what got into you?" Kiana said.

He didn't know how to answer. What had he done now?

She tilted her head. "Lionel! Joke!"

He didn't get it, but he laughed. "Yeah. Sorry. I'm a bit spaced
after the run. You guys stop at the lights?"

"No."

"I meant, at any of the lights …?"

She grinned. "No."

She was acting weird again.

He crossed his arms. "I guess I'll get my stuff and hustle back
home. What classes you got today?"

"Same as every Thursday: English, art, science, and geography
— and gym."

Stupid question — even for him.

Deepak, Afonso, and Georgina came back as a pack.

"This might sound totally ridiculous, but I almost like running," Deepak said. "It's like I miss it when we don't meet. There's
something wrong with my brain."

"I could've told you that," Afonso said.

Deepak narrowed his eyes. "Words can hurt," he said.

Lionel forced out a laugh. Deepak said it to be funny, but it was true. Words hurt on the inside, way more than getting punched or kicked.

"Are we going to run again tomorrow?" Georgina said.

"I'm in," Deepak said. "I need to beat Lionel once."

They all laughed. Lionel knew they didn't mean to diss him bad.

"Don't you think Lionel should try out for the track team?" Kiana said. "We have a practise after school today."

There she went again — relentless.

"You should," Georgina said. "You're so fast. I mean, do you even get tired?"

"I do … I just … I was full of energy today. Normally, I don't go that fast," Lionel said.

"You should definitely go out, bro," Deepak said.

"You're a natural runner," Afonso said. "I've been reading about it."

"You can read?" Deepak said.

"The article had pictures," Afonso said. "Lionel, you run easy, no effort. The article said some people are built to run. They have a perfect running motion, efficient. I think you're like that."

"I'm too fat to be a runner," Lionel said.

To his horror they all stared back at him, disapprovingly.

"You should at least try," Georgina said quietly. "You're the fastest one here, and with a little practise and more runs … you'll be great, and … it would be something to do after school …"

"You got us all running, not to mention getting our dads to get off their butts and fix up their stores," Deepak said.

"Not to mention getting me out of my black boots and into real running shoes," Georgina said.

"Which are black," Deepak said.

"Kinda goes with the outfit," Georgina said, and she struck a modelling pose.

"Not to mention how you helped my dad," Kiana said.

"We all helped you with that," Lionel said.

He needed to go. This was so uncomfortable. It's like no one in the world could ever just leave him alone. He liked to run, and he beat Bryan in a stupid race, but he was hardly track team material. He'd look like a blimp compared to the other kids. Time to put an end to this.

"I'll think about it," he said. He didn't want to lie to them. They weren't exactly friends, but they were the closest thing to friends he had. "Anyway, I gotta get back to my place. I forgot to ask my mom something. Sorry. I'll get my sweatshirt from inside …"

He was rambling.

Lionel made himself smile and went inside the empty café to get his sweatshirt. Binny had used the marble table for the milk, cream, sugar, and cup lids. It looked nice against the wall. He'd also hung the chandelier. It was beautiful, especially when it was all lit up. Then he noticed the old photos. Binny had framed them and scattered them about. They made the place feel cozy, more relaxed.

"Why do you do that?" Kiana said from behind, her voice quivering ever so slightly.

He gripped his sweatshirt in both hands and turned around slowly to face her.

"I'm not sure … Do what?"

Kiana dropped her head and raised her eyes. "You're always putting yourself down and … like calling yourself fat, and not wanting to run when you're an awesome runner and you should come out for the team. And you never take credit for anything good that you do, although I get it's good to be modest about stuff. I get that." She pressed her lips together. "I don't get you, though — at all."

"Nothing to get," he said.

He was just Lionel — some fat kid who got mad and won a stupid race.

She shook her head. Her eyes tightened. "You need to be the Lionel who picked himself off the track and dusted Bryan like he wasn't even there. That was you, in case you forgot. That's what you can do when you try. And your story was awesome. Why'd you wait so long to read it out? Everyone else read theirs. It's okay to be shy. Like I said, nothing wrong with modest. But you take it to an all-time level."

"I'm ... sorry," he stammered.

"What are you sorry about?" she yelled, tossing her hands up.

"I ... don't know, but you're mad at me."

"I'm not mad at you. I'm frustrated with you and ... you're letting your life go by. What's wrong with you?"

Like Brent said. He was a Do-Nothing. "I'm sorry," he said, barely louder than a whisper.

He needed to go. His chest pain was back and he felt that sick feeling rising in his throat. He headed to the door.

"Like that's the solution," she said. "Run away and don't deal with things. You're the one who showed my dad to face his problems."

Lionel reached for the door handle.

"You're not even going to look at me when I'm talking?"

He turned. "I read my story. That's what you wanted. I did it, for you, and now I'm getting pummeled at school, and it'll get worse if I run track. Trust me. It's not your fault. I did it to myself. But what do you want from me?"

Tears formed in the corners of Kiana's eyes.

"I gotta go," he said.

He pushed the door open. She pushed it shut.

"Lionel, wait." Kiana smiled and shook the hair from her face. "I'm sorry. I'm being pushy, like I always am. You're right.

I shouldn't be telling you to do something you don't want to do. Sorry. Forget it. Anyway, that's not what I wanted to talk to you about. I wanted to ask what you're doing tomorrow."

What was she going on about?

"Tomorrow? Usual — going to school. Did we decide if we were running in the morning?" Lionel said.

"I meant after school ... at night?"

"Um ... nothing. Not sure. Probably nothing."

"Good!" She clapped her hands lightly. "Come to Rashmi's. She's having a party, not a big deal, just some kids. You know everyone. It'll be fun — and you said you weren't doing anything."

He didn't know where to look. He was never invited to parties.

"I'm ... not much of a party guy," he said.

She tilted her head and lowered her eyelids. "Not a huge surprise. But ... it won't kill you to come out. I want you to. We're just hanging out, talking, listening to some music. No big deal. Come for a little bit."

"Well ... maybe. I'm not sure what my mom's doing."

She laughed. "Okay, if you're not going to spend the night with your mommy, then come by at eight or so."

"I ... don't know where she lives."

"I'll text you the address," she giggled. "It's close to school. I'd go with you, but I'm helping Rashmi set things up and stuff."

His knees felt weak. "Okay. Maybe. Anyway, I gotta go ... like I said. I'll see you at school."

"And tomorrow night," she said.

He mumbled a "goodbye" and left.

Lionel still couldn't believe he was here. He was actually standing in front of Rashmi's house. The two Lionels had gone to war,
with Kiana texting him ten times telling him he had to come.
Finally, he said yes. He wasn't sure why. Did he want to, or was
he scared of Kiana somehow? Why would he be afraid of someone half his size? She couldn't beat him up, and she never yelled
at him, except maybe yesterday morning in the café.

The sweat was dripping down his neck. That's what this party
needed, a fat, drippy, smelly loser. He dug a tissue out of his pocket and wiped the sweat off. He rubbed his cheek with his upper
arm, a trick he'd learned to see if his armpits smelled without
looking like he was sniffing them. He'd gone crazy with the
deodorant. His heart was sure pounding hard enough, worse
than when he ran. He felt so calm when he ran.

Why go to a party if it made you sick?

But he'd promised Kiana.

He was scared of her. He might as well admit it.

Lionel crossed the street. Rashmi lived in a nice house. She
could walk to school. It had dark red brick, two storeys, with a
big porch out front, and stairs leading up to the door. He stopped
at the stairs and took another deep breath. Kiana would be happy
to see him. He'd show her he wasn't afraid of showing up. He'd
do it for her.

"Okay … um … you sorta have to be invited," Nick said.

Bryan and Mohamed followed Nick up the driveway. Lionel gripped the handrail. Nick kept coming until he was almost nose-to-nose with him.

"Didn't I tell you not to mess with me — like that time you threw Kiana's note on the floor in math?" Nick said. "That was a smooth move. Kiana was seriously mad at me. Cost me a bundle at Pearl's to apologize." He pushed Lionel in the chest. "You should pay me back for that. You owe me twelve bucks."

"I ..."

"I ... I ... I ..." Nick chanted.

Lionel took a step back.

"This idiot tossed a note from Kiana onto the floor," Nick said. "Mr. Bore saw it. He freakin' read it out in class and Kiana was all over me, like it was my fault that this loser can't throw a piece of paper two feet onto a desk."

"He didn't exactly read it out," Lionel said.

Nick charged and smashed a forearm into his chest. Lionel tripped over a low hedge and fell to the ground.

"Hey, Nick-man. Let's be cool," Mohamed said.

"I am cool, Mo," Nick said. "This stiff owes me twelve bucks. I want it. Make it fifteen, with interest."

He had twenty dollars in his pocket. "I can pay you on Monday, at school," he said.

He'd stay home and maybe Nick would forget.

"Make it twenty," Nick sneered. "I'll take Kiana out again."

Lionel groaned inwardly and got back up. He reached into his pocket for the money.

"What are you doing here, anyway?" Nick said.

"Kiana invited me," Lionel said.

Nick's eyes got bigger, and then he burst out laughing. Bryan and Mohamed laughed a bit, but not too hard.

"I can't believe she pulled it off. I owe Kiana five bucks," Nick said.

"What for?" Bryan said.

"She bet me she could get Lionel to show up at Rashmi's party," Nick said. He shook his head as if in disbelief. "I told her no way he'd show — but here he is."

Lionel head began to spin. "Why would she ...?"

"You gotta come in," Nick said. "Kiana will laugh her head off. This is perfect. Bro — do you even know anyone here? Seriously? You're like the perfect brainless loser. I thought Stephane was clueless. You're the King of Clueless."

The front door opened. Kiana and Rashmi came onto the porch. Kiana was laughing and she waved.

"Hi, Lionel. I knew you'd come," Kiana said.

Lionel stared up in horror. That was why she'd sent those texts.

Lionel raced across the lawn.

"Green Machine, come back," Nick shouted. "I want those shoes."

He ran down the sidewalk, pumping his fists to push himself faster and faster.

*Get away.*

*Run.*

Lionel turned the corner and headed down the street. His breathing got regular and he slowed into his usual pace. The bus stop was to his right, but he kept going straight. He needed to run, and so he kept going and going, weaving his way through the streets until he was at the top of the Market. He finally stopped, hands on his knees, trying to catch his breath. His chest heaved painfully. He'd never run so hard for so long.

Lionel walked along the familiar street, but it felt very different: alien, cold, unwelcome. He passed Adler Shoes. He'd been working hard with Rajeev to fix it up. They'd put in a new floor, and a front desk, and some shelving. He'd also helped organize the stock room, labelling everything so they could find the shoes faster. Deepak said this morning that his dad was like a new person, excited about the store and how it looked.

"For the first time, he's proud of it," Deepak had said.

Lionel could tell Deepak was proud of it, too.

He stopped across from Big Ray's. Since his mom started him on the Runner's Diet he hadn't had a single slice of pizza, or a burger, or ice cream. He'd eaten a salad with baked chicken before heading out to Rashmi's. He was starving after running home, though. He crossed the street. The smell was so intense his mouth began to water. He needed a treat — one slice. After what happened tonight, he deserved it.

"Li – o – nel," Big Ray called out from behind a steel counter. He was rolling out some pizza dough. "Haven't seen or heard from you in ages. I thought you'd turned on me. All I see is you running past me every day."

"Sorry — I was running a bit, for fun, nothing important. Kinda stupid, but it was fun."

"No need to say sorry. Good for a kid to work out. You run for the track team?" Big Ray said.

Lionel shook his head. "I'm too slow for that."

"You okay?" Big Ray said.

Lionel felt like he might cry. He blinked rapidly. "I was running and ... I have some sweat in my eyes," he said.

"Here's some paper towel," Big Ray said. "No worries."

Lionel turned away and wiped the tears aside. The smell of the pizza dough was overwhelming, almost sickeningly sweet, like he was covered in flour. He coughed a few times. He had twenty dollars to spend.

"I'll have a two-litre Coke," he said, "and a party-size pizza, with extra sausage, onions, peppers, and double cheese."

"Coming right up," Big Ray said. "You having a party?"

"Yeah, my mom has some friends coming," he lied.

His mom had a bookkeeping class, and then she said she was going out for a drink with some of the other students. She had to write a test tomorrow morning, and this was the last class for the first course.

It would be a party of one.

"Help yourself to the drink from the fridge," Big Ray said. "It'll be a few minutes for the pizza. Is this delivery or are you going to wait?"

"I'll wait," he said.

Lionel sat on a stool and stared out the window trying to ignore the massive knot in his stomach. He was so hungry he could barf. Ridiculously hungry. It had been so long since he'd eaten something good. Pasta and chicken and rice and vegetables — enough already. Stupid, this running thing. Jumbo the Elephant lumbering along the sidewalk in stupid green shoes. So stupid.

"What's up with the running? You in training for something?" Big Ray said.

"Nope. Something to do. Not doing it much anymore."

Big Ray spun the dough in the air. Lionel took a big sip of Coke. It burned the back of his throat. He took another drink and kept drinking until half the bottle was gone. Big Ray was laughing.

"You're one thirsty dude," he chuckled.

"I guess," Lionel said.

He wanted to finish it right then and there, but Big Ray would think he was weird.

The door opened and two men walked in. One of them turned and grinned broadly.

"Check it out, Fergus. It's my ol' buddy, Lionel. How you keeping?"

Brent stumbled slightly and reached out and grabbed Fergus to steady himself.

"You look a bit different," Brent said.

He was slurring his words. Lionel figured he and Fergus had spent some time at the Uptown.

"You're not nearly as fat as you used to be. You working out?" Brent burped and he began to laugh.

"Not really," Lionel said.

He turned his head away. Brent's breath was rancid.

"Yo, Big Ray. Two of your freshest slices, my good sir," Brent said.

Fergus leaned against the wall, his chin on his chest.

"You and Charlene having another pizza dinner?" Brent said.

"I guess."

"Tell your mom the job is going great," Brent said.

"Okay."

Brent craned his neck and looked out the window. "Foster and Tanner are heading over. Let's scarf these and go back," he said to Fergus.

Fergus shrugged and folded his arms. Lionel thought he might actually be trying to sleep standing up.

"Tell your mom I bought a car, too," Brent said. "Brand new one. Fergus and I are gonna go down south when winter hits. We get tons of vacation."

"Here are the slices, boys," Big Ray said.

"Pay the man," Brent said to Fergus.

Fergus awoke with a start and stumbled to the cash. Brent grabbed his slice. He folded it in half and took a massive bite. Tomato sauce dripped down his chin.

"Tell your mom ... I'm with someone, a young beautiful girl, so she shouldn't get her hopes up about me coming back." Brent poked Lionel in the arm. "Tell her she can forget that."

Lionel couldn't look at him.

Brent poked his arm. "Tell her, okay?"

Lionel looked out the window. A couple of guys were yelling at someone outside the Uptown.

"Foster and Tanner are getting into it," Brent said. "C'mon Fergus." He grabbed Fergus by the arm and pulled him outside.

Lionel put his hands between his knees and slumped down. He was tired from his run. Stupid thing to do. Bus was right there.

"Hey, Lionel. Your pizza is ready," Big Ray said.

Lionel got off the stool and pulled his money out.

Big Ray shook his head and held the box up. "Don't worry about it. Glad to see you back. This is on me. Say hi to your mom."

"Thanks," Lionel said quietly.

"Don't let him bother you," Big Ray said. "He's had a few tonight. He gets like that."

"He doesn't bother me," Lionel said. "Bye."

"You take care," Big Ray said.

Lionel headed home. He walked past the café. The lights were out. Manuel had closed up the garage also. Everyone was home. Deepak and Afonso were probably at a party. They were popular kids. He continued along until he hit a red light. Cars whizzed by and he had to wait. The pizza smelled good, especially the sausage.

The traffic cleared and he crossed. A few minutes later, his building came into view. He scanned for any Hombres and then jogged across the street.

"Hey, bro. Spare a brother some pizza," a man's voice rang out.

He stepped out of the shadows, the same man who'd stolen his money.

Lionel gripped the box tightly. If he was going to eat this all himself, he needed to make a run for it now.

The man rubbed his hands together and grinned. "What kind did ya order, boy?"

Lionel looked down at the pizza. This wasn't him anymore. He was a runner.

"Take it," Lionel said. "And you can have the rest of the Coke."

"Thanks, brother. You want a piece?"

"I'm not hungry."

Lionel walked slowly to the elevators.

He sighed and shook his head. The elevator wasn't coming — or it was broken again, more like it. He started up the stairs, two at a time. The third-floor landing had garbage stuffed in the corner and a bunch of beer bottles lined up on the stairs. He pushed the door open for his floor, stormed into his apartment, and immediately turned his console on.

He got through the first two sections easily and headed up the castle hill. The dragon would come from the right and he readied the ranger with a grenade launcher.

He was hungry, but he ignored the pangs and kept playing. The dragon flew down and the ranger let the grenade go. The dragon burst into flames and the ranger jumped over the moat filled with alligators and charged into the castle. A mass of demons grinned at him from the top of the stairs. The ranger sprayed them with machine-gun fire, and soon the floor was littered with demon parts.

"Too bad, so sad," Lionel said.

Some owls scurried past and he collected them for points. He'd be at the top of the tower soon. He had to jump down, and then he'd be facing the skeletons, the ogre, and the vultures. The controller was working fine now. He felt unstoppable.

Why couldn't life always be like this? He'd run and game. What else did he need?

The two skeletons ran at him from behind a tree, their bones rattling. He made short work of them with a vicious sweep of his sword. The ogre then made his mad charge across the field. The ranger pulled out his machine gun. He jumped on his horse and set off in a gallop. The ogre jumped.

"Yeah, baby!" Lionel cried with glee.

He'd cut the ogre in two with a hail of bullets to his midsection. The ogre lay on the ground, blood seeping from him. Lionel made the horse rear back, the ranger shaking his gun in triumph. The vultures were calling out in their hideous voices, but he knew they'd never reach him in time. He pushed the button and the ranger took off into the forest. He paused the game. He wasn't feeling that well — kinda queasy. Maybe he should eat something. He burped. Probably drank the Coke too fast. He burped again. He felt sick.

He un-paused the game and the ranger started riding through the forest, but ten seconds later, he had to pause it again. He was going to be sick. Made no sense. He hadn't eaten the pizza. He ran to the washroom and dropped to his knees.

## Sunday: 9:00 a.m.

A light crossed his face and Lionel groaned. He opened his eyes.

"Lionel, honey? I wanted to check on you."

He groaned again and rolled onto his side.

"Do you still have that migraine?" his mom said.

"Yeah, a little," he mumbled.

He didn't really, but he also didn't want to get out of bed. His mom would believe he was sick so he could miss school next week; then he had to pray they'd forget about him. He'd spent half the night trying to figure out how he could get transferred out of English and math. He would quit school rather than be there with Kiana or Nick. He was serious this time. He didn't care what Ryder said, or Whellan, or anyone.

"I'm sorry about yesterday." His mom came over, sat on the edge of his bed, and began to stroke his hair.

He closed his eyes.

"I had that bookkeeping test. I felt bad about leaving you for that long."

"I just slept," he said.

"Poor thing. Did you take a pill?"

He shook his head.

"Okay ... but take one if you need to. Anyway, after class I went out for coffee with someone from the class, so that was why I was a bit late."

He opened his eyes. "Who'd you go with?"

"A friend … from class."

"A guy friend?"

"Yes, Lionel, a guy friend. But don't worry, not another Brent. He's nice. He has two kids. His wife passed away a few years ago and he wants a job where he doesn't have to work such long hours. He was in construction."

Lionel closed his eyes again. "I saw Brent on Friday."

"Okay."

"He told me to tell you he has a new car and a new girlfriend."

She sighed. "Good for him."

"I think he'd been drinking at the Uptown."

"Not a surprise. Let's forget about him." She sighed again and began stroking his hair. "Actually, let's not. I'm embarrassed about that, and I shouldn't have put you through it. I was so down, so sad, not sure why, and he was someone who happened to be around. I know it sounds pathetic, but I guess I thought any man is better than no man. Definitely wrong. Anyway, we went to Binny's Café. I finally got there. It's such a great place, and when I told them I was your mother, they made such a fuss over me and wouldn't let me pay for anything — and they showed me the room you cleaned up. My goodness, they're big Lionel fans over there."

He raised himself on one elbow. "Not all of them," he said.

His mom's eyes narrowed. "They did mention something about Friday night. You left a party?"

"I was feeling sick."

"They sounded a bit worried," she said.

He lay back. Kiana had texted him, but he wasn't falling for it again. Deepak and Afonso had texted a few times too, asking where he was.

"Poor Lionel. Are you hungry?"

"I could eat."

Truth was he'd been so upset about the party he'd barely eaten yesterday. He was starving, actually.

"How about a little hot cereal?"

He nodded.

"Anyway, let's get out of that bed, and it wouldn't kill you to take a shower — and if you're not up for a run, at least you should take a walk. You could visit your friends at Binny's. Some fresh air would be good, even if you have a headache. Might make it better. You shouldn't be cooped up in this bedroom for another day."

He was getting bored, but he sure wasn't going to Binny's! Kiana must've told her parents the story and they'd misunderstood it as him just leaving the party. It made him sad to think he'd never see Binny and Gwen again. They were nice people. He'd also never see Deepak or Afonso or Georgina.

"I'll get up, Mom," he said. "Give me a sec."

She patted his arm and left. Lionel swung his feet out of bed. He felt a bit dizzy and the headache was still there, but not as bad as before. He actually felt pretty good. Maybe he would go for that run. A shower was a good idea. He hadn't taken one after running home Friday.

He took a quick shower, dressed, and sat down to eat. He was so hungry he felt sick.

"So ... I was speaking to Gwen," his mom said, sitting down with him. "She told me you organized the running club, the Marketeers, and also you've been helping out at the shoe store and the garage, and that you've done a great job."

He didn't need to be reminded of the Marketeers.

"She also told me how much your work upstairs meant to her family and how much happier Binny is," she said.

Lionel shrugged. "All I did was throw out some broken furniture."

She hesitated. "Are you going to take that walk?" she said.

"Maybe later. I'll game a bit," he said.

He didn't want to blow his cover.

"Why don't you walk first?"

"Don't feel like it."

"Lionel, it's not healthy."

"It's Sunday. I'm ... still kinda tired."

"You were in bed all day yesterday."

"I know."

"Lionel, are you ... Is something wrong? You're not ... yourself."

"I'm just sick. No big deal."

She rubbed his arm. "You know you can tell me anything." She paused. "Are you feeling a little ... anxious? Maybe you should take one of your pills. Remember, the doctor said you shouldn't wait until you're really upset. I could set up an appointment next week."

She wasn't going to leave him alone. "Okay, how about I go for a quick walk and see if I feel better," he said. "I don't need a pill, honest."

She leaned over and gave him a kiss. "Promise to tell me if you're not ... feeling yourself. It's okay to admit it. There's nothing to be ashamed about."

"I will. Thanks."

"Do you want more cereal?"

He shook his head and went to get changed. She began to clean up. He threw on some sweatpants and a hoodie and left.

The recycling was gone from the hallway. He felt bad about that. Donna must've done it herself. He'd messed up.

He waited for the elevator for a minute.

"As usual," he muttered, and headed for the stairwell.

"Lionel, there you are," Donna called out.

She had a bag slung across her shoulder — and she was limping badly.

"Are … you okay?" he asked.

She waved him off. "It's nothing. I'm so clumsy. I was carrying out some recycling yesterday and I fell. What do you kids say, *my bad*?"

That didn't help with the guilt.

"Sorry about that. I wasn't feeling well," he said.

"Your mom told me you were ill. Don't worry about it. It's good to see you're feeling better," she said.

The elevator opened.

"A miracle," she laughed.

She began walking back, but she was moving very slowly. She was going to miss it.

"Ach. Being old is a pain." She waved her cane at the doors. They were closing.

Lionel slipped by her and threw his arm between the closing doors. They popped back open.

"My hero," Donna cried out. She walked in and gave his arm a squeeze. "Thanks. I probably would've had to wait another half an hour." She looked out. "Are you coming down or going back home?"

She'd seen him walking away from the elevators. "Go ahead. I have to talk to Mom."

She pointed at him. "You going for a run?"

"Um … yeah."

"How's the watch?"

She pointed at his wrist. He'd gotten into the habit of wearing it and had put it on without thinking when he finished his shower.

"It's great. Yeah … awesome. It keeps good time."

"Wonderful. I'm glad. Enjoy your run."

The doors closed. He had to laugh. The elevator finally comes and he can't take it.

"Hello stairs," he said out loud.

He headed over, rubbing the back of his neck. A walk was actually a good idea. He thought about the conversation with his mom in his bedroom, and what Brent had said to him. She wasn't the same person Brent knew. Whether it was talking to that Andrea woman, or this bookkeeping course, she'd changed. She was way happier and more positive. She'd started to cook — and bake — and sometimes he caught her singing to herself. She didn't even watch TV that much anymore.

She kept telling him he was the reason. That she saw him running, and getting in shape, and cleaning his bedroom, and decided she hadn't been a good mother, and that she felt especially bad about letting Brent into their lives. Lionel couldn't help but wonder if this new guy didn't have something to do with her feeling better.

At least one of them was doing well.

He checked that Donna wasn't in the lobby. He didn't want to run into her again. Then he'd have to lie about why he didn't take the elevator. The coast was clear and he left. When he stepped outside he heard a bang. Donna was recycling. He ran in the opposite direction as fast as he could.

"Lionel! Yo! Wait up."

Georgina waved from across the street. She wore black leggings and a black top with a zipper in the front. He had no choice but to slow down. She ran over to him.

"Hey, Georgina. How're the muscles today?" Lionel said.

That was their private joke. She was skin and bones.

"Sore and ready to go," she said, like always.

Something was different about her today. Lionel took a closer look. "Your earrings … and your other stuff," he said. "Did you lose them?" She wasn't wearing her piercings. She only had one pair of earrings, and they were normal. Then he noticed her hair had been cut shorter and wasn't as black. She was almost like a new person.

She laughed nervously and tucked her hair behind her ears. "I decided to tone it down a bit. I don't want to terrorize the customers."

"It suits you," Lionel said. "Looks good — not that you didn't look good before," he hurried to add.

"You're sweet to say that," she said. "But I get it. Maybe I was overdoing the Goth a bit. Do I need twenty-five earrings, two nose piercings, and one in my tongue?"

Lionel agreed, but he wasn't going to say it. Fortunately, she continued.

"I started dressing Goth in high school. I went to a new school in grade nine. I had no friends, not that I had a ton in my primary school, which made it kinda scary. I tried fitting in and meeting people, or maybe I only pretended too, but anyway, before long I was kinda alone, eating by myself all the time, hanging in the library at lunch, all those cliché things. It was definitely not a good time. Got worse when a few of the girls decided it was fun to pick on me. I noticed there was one group of kids that no one picked on — the Goth kids. They hung out at the front of the school and smoked cigarettes when the teachers weren't looking. I bought myself some black clothes and black boots and pierced my ears, and one day, I just joined them. For a week no one talked to me; they didn't tell me to leave either, and eventually they just accepted me. After that I kept going until I was hard core."

Lionel listened intently. He knew all about trying to fit in.

"I don't think the other Goths really liked me, but it's not like there were hundreds of kids trying to get into their little club;

you're basically in as long as you wear the right clothes. Not all the Goths were self-destructive, but some were, and we began drinking by the end of grade ten and then ... well ... then I lost interest in school and began failing. I acted like I didn't care, and dropped out when I was sixteen. My parents and I were basically fighting all the time by then, and I got tired of it, and my parents got tired of my behavior and staying out late. Anyway, I started working at the café when I was seventeen and moved out."

"Well ... I guess you're doing okay then," he said.

She made a sour face. "Not sure of that. Since we've been running, I don't know, I've started thinking about my life," Georgina said. "It's like running is the only time I think clearly, without distractions. I like running with the Marketeers, but I think better when I'm on my own. Does that make sense?"

He nodded.

"I started running at night — long runs," Georgina continued. "Not fast like you, but long, and I just think about things, how I feel, whether I'm happy or not, my family." Georgina tucked a stray strand of hair behind her ear. "I've made some bad decisions, I think, and it started with me dropping out of school. I'm thinking that maybe I'm still letting those girls bully me. They made me change the way I dress, the way I talked, and acted, and then they made me quit school." She looked at Lionel closely. "I guess I'm tired of being afraid."

She began bouncing lightly from foot to foot. "Were you sick? We went for a good run yesterday. Kiana said you were at some party and left."

"That's what she said?" He'd had enough of Kiana's garbage.

"Not exactly. She invited me to a party and ... she bet Nick, this guy, that she could get me there ... for five bucks, and ... she thought it would be funny."

Georgina stopped bouncing. "Not understanding you. What are you talking about?"

"Kiana, she tricked me into coming to that stupid party — to make me look dumb in front of everyone."

"Why would she do that?"

"So everyone would laugh at the fat loser who wasn't actually invited?"

She stared up at him. "I'm a little confused. You said Kiana invited you to the party."

"Yeah."

"So how is it that you weren't invited?"

"She invited me because Nick didn't believe she could get me to show up. I obviously wasn't invited — no one wanted me there. They all think I'm a joke. Kiana bet she could make me come. I never go out. I never get invited to parties, not even birthday parties when I was a little kid. It's like what you said …" He felt a rush of emotion and he struggled to keep calm. "I don't ever fit in, and … Anyway, she got me there, and, of course, everyone was laughing at me because … they knew about the bet and …"

He had to turn away. His eyes were burning. The memory of Kiana coming out of the house flooded back — and in that instant, he saw his father staring at him, mocking him.

*Three strikeouts. You're useless.*

His dad's voice echoed in his head.

"Lionel?"

He practically jumped out of his skin. "Sorry, I was …"

"I don't know what happened," Georgina said quietly. "I obviously wasn't there. But I don't think Kiana would do that — especially to you. I … I can't see it. She likes you, more than you think."

Georgina pulled him by the elbow so he was facing her.

"I know all about hiding from people," she said. "I do it differently than you. I hide behind my Goth armor. It's like I'm saying, 'Don't mess with me. I'm dressed in black and I'm covered in skulls and tattoos and piercings. You can't hurt me. I'm too tough.'"

A tear fell down her cheek.

"You hide by not getting involved," she continued. "You literally hide from people so you won't be hurt. You don't go out, you don't make friends, and you put yourself down."

"You don't know me," he said, barely louder than a whisper. "I'm … nothing. I'm just here. Other than my mom, who cares what I do?"

"I care."

"You're being nice, but … what about every kid at school …?"

"Lionel, you drive me crazy. You drive us all crazy. You're an awesome kid and you've done so much to help people, like me," Georgina said. "You invited me to run with the Marketeers. No one else even thought of me. Only you. The Marketeers …" She was crying now. "They're maybe the first friends I've had who just accepted me, who didn't care what I wore and what I looked like. You helped Binny get over his hoarding, and Deepak and Afonso to get in shape, and Rajeev to fix Adler Shoes — and Manuel to fix up his garage. How can you say no one cares? We do, and we're all worried about you. Deepak and Afonso sent you texts and wanted to go to your place. But we didn't know where you live …" Her voice trailed off for a moment. "Do you live nearby?"

"Yeah, in that apartment."

He pointed to the building.

She reached out and gave him a hug. He felt awkward about it — she was a few years older — but he hugged her back. At least he had one friend.

"Keep believing in yourself," she said. "You're better than you give yourself credit for, and you're a Marketeer, so don't even think about not running with us. And you're wrong about Kiana. I can't believe she would do that. Maybe you misunderstood something ... I don't know this Nick guy, but would she really do that for him?"

She had a point there. Kiana had told him Nick wasn't her boyfriend — and the notes seemed to irritate her more often than not.

Georgina scrunched her mouth to the side. "Talk to her. I bet you have it wrong."

"I don't think so."

She grinned. "She's at the café right now. She told me she was doing some homework. Let's ask."

"I'm not ..."

"Chicken?"

"No. I just ..."

She began making clucking noises. He tried not to laugh. It was impossible not to. Then he got mad again.

"I'm not going. Whatever. It doesn't matter. Kiana and I are ... we were ... I don't know what we were, but who cares? It's not like she does."

"That's it. You're talking such garbage, it's ridiculous. You and I are going to the café right now."

"Georgina!"

"Either that, or I'm bringing her to your apartment." She laughed. "You look like you're going to faint, Lionel. Trust me on this. Let's talk to her. What's the worst that can happen? She laughs at you. You can run out of the café and never come back. But don't you want to know for sure?"

He did more than she'd ever know. Was it possible he'd misunderstood?

He groaned. "This is gonna be painful."

Georgina grinned. "Let's run, then. Take your mind off it."

"I'll be all sweaty."

"It's less than ten minutes away. That's not even a warmup for you."

He took a deep breath. "Okay. A little more humiliation can't hurt me. But you have to come with me."

"Of course," she said. "Oh, and one more thing. If you're wrong about Kiana, you have to try out for the track team. Deal?" She held her hand out.

He shook her hand without thinking about it.

All he could think about was Kiana.

Despite all that had happened, he still wanted to see her. A little humiliation would be worth it. Humiliation he could take. He was an expert on that.

He set off beside Georgina as they settled into an easy pace.


## Sunday: 10:15 a.m.

Fear he knew — but never like this. The café door seemed like a massive castle gate, and the sidewalk an alligator-filled moat, like in his video game. He barely remembered running here. His mind had gone blank. He couldn't imagine what he'd say.

"We sorta ... gotta go in ... if you want to talk to her," Georgina said.

He groaned again.

She laughed and began to push him. Her hands were so tiny. He was a mountain compared to her.

"Okay, okay. I'll go," he said.

He stepped inside. It was fairly busy. A line of people snaked along the counter waiting to order. Binny was standing behind the espresso machine.

"Lionel! Bro! How are ya?"

"I'm good, Binny."

The people in line turned to look at him.

"A day off and you can't stay away from me?" Binny said to Georgina.

"You're irresistible," Georgina said. "I needed to see your face. I also need to deliver Lionel. Is Kiana here?"

"Kiana and Rashmi are in the corner," Binny said. "I heard you were sick, Lionel. Was it like a twenty-four-hour flu?"

"Something like that, I guess. I'm okay now."

"Two mango-banana smoothies, then?" Binny laughed.

"Can you make mine a latté?" Georgina said.

"Consider it done," Binny said. He turned away to the coffee grinder before Lionel could object.

"To the corner," Georgina whispered.

"I didn't know Rashmi was here," he said.

"Neither did I," Georgina said. "Now man up and talk to her."

He walked over, barely feeling the floor under his feet.

Kiana saw him coming. Her face turned serious and she waved him over.

"What happened?" Kiana said. "You just ran off, and then you didn't come out for our run yesterday. I've texted you twenty times, and so did Deepak and Afonso. You didn't answer once."

"I wasn't feeling well," he said.

"But … why …?" Her voice broke. "What's going on, Lionel? I was so worried I didn't sleep last night."

She was exaggerating, obviously. She didn't worry about anything. What could she be worried about?

"Ask," Georgina said, poking him in the ribs.

He glared at her.

"Don't give me the eyes," Georgina said. "You ask or I will — and get ready for that tryout."

"Ask what?" Kiana said. "And what tryout?"

Georgina gripped Lionel's forearm. "Out with it."

Lionel quieted his nerves. It couldn't get worse. His reputation was mud at school anyway. Nick and his crew were going to chirp him forever.

"Nick told me," he blurted.

That didn't get the reaction he expected. Kiana screwed her eyes tightly and stared at him.

"He told me," he repeated.

"I'll ask the obvious question. Told you what?" Kiana said.

Lionel began to turn away. "I knew she'd ..."

Georgina stopped him. "Lionel thinks you bet some kid, this Nick, that you could trick Lionel into coming to the party so you could all make fun of him."

Kiana sat back in her seat. Tears formed in the corners of her eyes.

"Lionel, you've lost it," Rashmi said. "Kiana asked if she could invite you and I said sure, why not."

Kiana remained perfectly still. Two tears had fallen.

"He told me ... Nick ... that you bet five dollars ... to get me there ... to Rashmi's," Lionel said.

"There was no bet," Kiana said.

She wiped her tears. Her eyes were ablaze. Lionel felt them burn into him.

"I'm going to check on those smoothies," Georgina said.

"I'll help you," Rashmi said.

They both got up and went to the counter. Lionel sat at the table.

"You think I'm that kind of person?" Kiana said.

"I ... don't think ... It's ..."

"It's what?"

"Nick said ..."

"If Nick said I was a mass murderer would you believe him?"

"Obviously …"

"Obviously what?"

"Obviously not … I don't think … I …" He sat back and closed his eyes. "Nick said there was a bet and I believed him. I guess that's it."

She leaned forward. "Why would you think I'd do that … to you of all people?"

"I guess … It made some sense to me at the time."

"I don't understand you."

"You're so nice. You don't chirp people or gossip, even though you could because everyone likes you. You let me run with you guys, which is fun because … sometimes it's fun to run with other people and not by myself all the time. I don't know why you bother with me. I appreciate it, but I don't get it. You're the most popular girl in grade eight and I'm … me. I guess that's why I believed him."

He put his hands on the table and lowered his head.

"Lionel," she said softly.

He raised his head. She put her hand on his and looked into his eyes. "I'd never do that to you. You have to believe me."

He didn't know what to believe.

"I don't understand why you're so hard on yourself," she said. "You get so embarrassed if I say you're a fast runner, which you are. You won't accept that for some reason, like …" She leaned forward. "You're different from other boys. I can talk to you, and I feel like you understand me. All the time we've spent together has been …" She suddenly began to cry again.

Her hand was so soft and warm, like a piece of velvet.

"I'm sorry, Kiana," he began. "Nick got on me and I …" No point hiding the truth. "I've spent my life avoiding guys like

Nick — and I'm good at it. Guys don't bug me much because they don't notice me. Obviously they get on me a little, you can't really be invisible, but you sort of can. When you came out of the house, and I thought you'd bet Nick, I felt like I was in a spotlight and the only way out was to run. Nick somehow knows a person's weakness and goes for it … and it's like there's no way to fight back."

Lionel noticed Georgina and Rashmi were talking at the coffee counter.

"I wonder where those smoothies are?" he said.

"Do you remember when I said I wouldn't mind having a boyfriend, if he was the right boy?" She put her hands in her lap, slumped her shoulders. "Do you think … maybe … you would be the right boy?"

This was impossible. It couldn't be happening.

"Are you sure?" he said.

She straightened up. "No, Lionel, I'm just saying it because I'm that kind of girl."

"I'm sorry …"

She pointed her finger at him. "And you have to promise not to say sorry all the time. It bugs me. You don't have anything to be sorry for."

"It's a bad habit, I guess." He looked over to the counter again. "Those smoothies are taking forever."

"Lionel, a girl just asked you out and …"

"What does a guy say in this situation?" he said, helplessly.

She put both her hands on his. "Look at me," she said.

She was so beautiful.

Kiana gave him a gentle kiss, so soft, like a breath of warm air.

"I think you're a wonderful person, the kindest, nicest, most honest boy I've ever met, and I feel comfortable with you — and one day you're going to have to accept that," she said.

Georgina and Rashmi came back to the table. Each of them held two smoothies.

"Mango-strawberry-banana for Kiana," Rashmi said, handing it over to her.

"And one mango-banana smoothie for Lionel," Georgina said. They sat down, both grinning away.

"Shut up," Kiana said, laughing.

"You lost a bet," Georgina said to Lionel.

"What bet?" he said.

"How quickly you forget ... after one little kiss," Georgina giggled. "You said you'd try out for the track team if you were wrong about Kiana."

"You did?" Kiana beamed. "That's awesome. We have a practise on Monday after school."

"It's too late for me ..."

"You lost the bet," Georgina said. "Now drink up."

## Monday: 3:40 p.m.

Lionel pressed his back against the school wall and closed his eyes.

"Do it," he said to himself for the hundredth time.

Every time he tried to go to track practise, something held him back. He looked around the corner again. A few kids were sitting beside the track, stretching. He rolled his neck. He was being such a wuss. He'd told Kiana that he would come, and she made him tell Whellan after English. Whellan looked a bit surprised, but he said Lionel was welcome to come out for a run. Kiana had gone on about how fast he was, which was embarrassing. Some of the other kids had snickered, and he could only imagine the fat jokes once they were out of earshot.

He ran a hand over his stomach. It didn't hang over his belt anymore. He could even feel his ribs. He obviously wasn't thin, but maybe fat was a bit harsh.

He'd eaten lunch with Kiana and Rashmi in the cafeteria. It was the first time he'd eaten lunch with people. It was fun, and they'd joked around. Rashmi was nice. He'd never spoken to her until yesterday at the café, and they got along like old friends. She was funny too, in a dry sort of way.

A few more kids showed up at the track. He needed to do this. It hadn't been a bad day, surprisingly. Nick and Bryan didn't pay him much attention.

"Hey, Lionel, how's it going?"

Stephane had snuck up on him.

"Hi, Stephane. It's going okay, I guess. What about you? Um … like … What are you up to? Going home?"

"No, I want to do some homework. I like watching track practise while I'm working. Gives me something to do every once in a while." Stephane smiled and nodded at the track. "You should run with the team. I watched you race Bryan. Jaime and I couldn't believe how fast you are. You have a lot of natural talent."

"Thanks. I lost my temper. Went a bit mental."

"I think it's more that you're a fast runner," Stephane said.

Lionel figured he should compliment him back. "You did pretty good playing basketball in gym. You guys won."

"Ach, I'm useless," Stephane said. "I just pass the ball to Nick, and he scores. I'm completely uncoordinated. He takes it so seriously I have to laugh."

That awkward moment had come. It always did when he talked to someone — other than Kiana and the Marketeers.

"I probably should get going … and you have your home-work," Lionel said.

"Sure. Have a good day. See you tomorrow," Stephane said. He pulled on the strap of his backpack and nodded. "I'll get to it."

He took a few steps towards the track. Lionel could tell he still wanted to talk. They did have one thing in common — Nick. May as well ask the obvious question.

"Does Nick bug you a lot?" Lionel said.

Stephane stopped. "I guess. I'm used to it."

"You should talk to a teacher … or Ryder," Lionel said.

Not like he'd ever do that. All of a sudden Lionel couldn't understand why he'd put up with Nick, put up with all the bully-ing all these years. Why not talk to a teacher or the principal? Was it better to get picked on every day?

"Like I said, I'm used to it," Stephane said. "It doesn't bug me so much. Maybe a little, like when he's throwing things or snapping his towel or … I get that he doesn't like guys like me."

"I'm not one to give advice on this, and Nick gets after me too, but I don't think we should take it because he thinks he has the right to chirp at guys," Lionel said.

This was most definitely the new Lionel talking.

"All I'm saying is … I've had it with him," Lionel said, "and Bryan and Mohamed, although those two aren't nearly so bad. Maybe … we should see Ryder together … or with Jaime, too. We could talk to Whellan …"

Stephane got very quiet.

Lionel was still afraid of Nick. He always would be. He was still afraid of Brent and the Hombres — and his dad. He just liked the new Lionel more than the old one — a lot more.

"I was thinking about it last night," Lionel said. "How we get bullied by guys and we never say anything. What if we did?"

Stephane tugged on his backpack straps again. "I'd like that," he said. "I'll speak to Jaime. I know he's tired of it. We can talk tomorrow?"

"Sounds good."

Stephane smiled, gratefully. He nodded and turned to leave, then stopped. "Thanks, Lionel. I feel a lot better. Nice to know someone cares." He gave Lionel another friendly nod and walked off.

Lionel felt a nasty rumble in his stomach. There weren't that many people at the track yet. Kiana said practise didn't really get going until four o'clock. Better go to the washroom in case his stomach needed … relief. And at the back of his head, down at the bottom, he sensed a headache coming on. Was he getting sick right before the practise? Brutal. He was the unluckiest person in the world.

No time to think about that. He needed a toilet.

Lionel went back inside the school. He looked around to make sure no one was watching and went into the washroom and slipped into his usual stall. He sat and waited. Sometimes it took a long time.

Not this time. Gross. Like diarrhea. Yuck.

His stomach wasn't going to let him off the hook so easy, either. At least he hadn't gone straight to the track. The kids would call him Poopy Pants Lionel if he had to race off to the toilet.

The washroom door opened. He heard talking, which meant more than one person. No one used this washroom after school. He cursed his bad luck. Now he'd have to stay until they left.

"I pull a muscle and he keeps chirping at me. He should race the guy if he's so fast."

Bryan! Great. He prayed they wouldn't notice him.

"You know what he's like. I feel sorry for that Lionel guy, though. I told Nick to chill, but he wants to kill him."

Mohamed!

And Nick wanted to kill him!

"How freaky is it that Kiana's going out with the guy?" Bryan said. "I'm like … okay … you're not into Nick, but Lionel?"

"Nick's lost it," Mohamed said. "He's in love with Kiana."

They moved to the sink.

"You know the freakiest thing?" Bryan said. "Lionel is super fast."

"Who? Lionel?"

"I'm telling you. The dude can run. It's insane. He's kinda fat, but not as fat as he used to be. He must be on a huge diet. I'm just saying, I had a lead on the guy and he caught up to me. I had a pulled muscle and couldn't run my fastest, but … it doesn't matter, and anyway, I gotta get to practise."

"What about your leg?"

"I'll go easy. I gotta be careful. The sectional meet is in three days."

The door opened. They were gone.

Lionel opened the stall door a crack and peeked out. Coast was clear. He went to the sink, washed his hands, and looked in the mirror. This two Lionels thing was stupid. He wasn't two people. Only one face looked back — one him.

Did he really want to hide in a washroom stall?

Kiana thought he was fast, and so did the Marketeers, and now Bryan.

He'd thought life was a lot easier in the shadows, where no one could see him. But it wasn't. The shadows made him sick and fat — and lonely. The shadows had him taking pills so he wouldn't freak out.

He knew what he had to do.

He looked into the mirror again. "Time for track practise, Mr. Fatso," he told himself.

He left and ran to the field before he could change his mind. There were about thirty kids huddled around Whellan. He slowed ten yards away. A few kids noticed him, including Bryan.

"Lionel! Hey! Over here. Told you he was coming, Mr. Whellan," Kiana said quickly.

Bryan watched him closely.

"Fantastic," Whellan said. "Have you thought about what race? This morning you said you liked long distance."

"He'd be perfect for the fifteen hundred," Kiana said.

Whellan laughed.

"The fifteen hundred sounds good," Lionel said. "I haven't thought about it. Kiana said I … Maybe I should've asked you first."

He almost apologized, but caught himself. Kiana gave him an encouraging smile.

"No worries," Whellan said. "We only have Bryan in the senior fifteen hundred, and we're allowed two runners. Why don't you join in with the others? We're just going to jog around the track?"

"Sounds good," Lionel said.

"Give me two laps, everyone," Whellan called out.

A few kids groaned.

"Even the field athletes need some cardio," Whellan chuckled. "And give me a good pace, please. We're hosting the sectional meet this Thursday. I want to qualify the entire team for the regionals, so we need good results from everyone."

They left in a big pack and headed into the first corner. Lionel followed along, but found the pace a little slow. By the back straightaway, he was in the middle of the pack. By the second turn, he was in front.

"It's two laps," he heard someone say sarcastically.

"Try keeping up with him," Lionel heard Kiana say.

"No one can keep that pace up," another kid said.

No choice now. He had to keep his pace up or they'd start chirping him — and Kiana. He didn't feel tired, so he pumped his hands harder and drove his knees up, pushing off with every stride. He felt a bit silly. The other kids would think he was showing off.

He wasn't going to disappoint Kiana, though.

"Go for it, Lionel," Whellan said. "I'm timing this lap. Go!"

Lionel glanced at his watch and put it in high gear. Dumb move not staying with the pack. Whellan had called it a warm up, not a sprint. That's why they were going slow. He was killing himself like an idiot. Up the back straightaway he went, then the corner, and then the front straightaway. Whellan held his stop-watch high overhead and brought it down when he passed.

"Lionel! That was awesome," Whellan said. "You took that

lap in … sixty-four seconds. Kiana was right. I think the fifteen hundred might be the perfect race for you."

Kiana and five of the older kids arrived together.

"Told ya," Kiana said jubilantly to Whellan.

"I'm impressed. Nice, easy stride," Whellan said. "Okay, come on guys," he yelled to the stragglers.

They waited for everyone to bring it in.

"Give me the field athletes in the middle of the field, please," Whellan said. "Sprinters, go down to the starting line and do your striding exercises. High knees first for a hundred meters and back with right and left shuffle steps. Do that twice. Distance runners, stay with me."

A hand touched Lionel's shoulder.

"I knew you'd come," Kiana said smugly.

Lionel flushed deeply.

"Don't be so serious, Lionel," she pouted. "Have fun. We'll talk after practise, okay?"

"Okay."

"I want to work on our pacing," Whellan said.

"Do you remember your one-lap target?" Whellan said. Lionel felt stupid being the only kid without a hand up. "Good. I want everyone to run two laps. I'll call out the time when you run by for the first lap. Keep to that target pace. You need to train your body to know when it's going the right speed." Whellan pointed at Lionel. "Lionel, let's shoot for a sixty-five second lap, and we'll go from there. Line it up," Whellan said.

A few kids hustled to take the inside lane. Lionel took a spot on the outside.

"My pulled muscle is still bugging me," Bryan said to Whellan.

"Can you run at all?" Whellan said.

"Yeah. It's not that bad. I just wanted to tell you … that I can't run my fastest," Bryan said.

"That guy always has an excuse for being slow," a boy next to Lionel said.

His friend laughed.

Lionel looked over at Bryan. He had that look on his face, the same look he had during their race, the look that said, "I'm scared."

Lionel readied himself. He wasn't scared.

Whellan turned from the whiteboard.

"So, do you see how the character connects to the dialogue? The kind of words you put in the character's mouth needs to match the character's personality."

The speakers overhead crackled.

"Sorry for the interruption," Mrs. Dempsey announced, "but can the members of the track team please make their way to the change room to get ready for the meet. Thank you — and good luck, team!"

Whellan nodded meaningfully at the door. "I believe we have three track members right here. Guys, get dressed and I'll be down in ten minutes when class is over."

Lionel got up with Kiana and Bryan.

"The juniors need to do better," Bryan said when they were out of the class. "Last year the grades one to four barely got any points and our team didn't make it through to the regionals."

"You make the regionals by either finishing in the top four in a final or your team wins the points competition in a sectional meet — then everyone on the team moves on," Kiana said to Lionel.

Lionel opened the door leading to the stairs. "How do you get team points?" he said.

"Top-ten finishers get points — first place ten, second place nine," Bryan said.

"Best thing is to focus on your own race and not worry about the points," Kiana said.

She was looking directly at Lionel.

How was he going to win? He'd never raced before.

"Easy for you to say," Bryan said. "Hamadi Kalu's running the fifteen hundred. He's won every cross-country event since he was a little kid, and he won the Citys last year."

"Lionel will beat him," Kiana said.

Bryan laughed. "Not sure about that."

She looked at Lionel again. "You'll win. I know it." She flicked her eyebrows. "See you out on the track."

She turned right to go to the girls' change room.

Lionel felt weird walking next to Bryan. They hadn't said a word to each other since their race.

"Did you run in the regionals last year?" Lionel asked, finally.

"I got a cold right before the meet — brutal. I could barely breathe," Bryan said.

"That's a drag."

"Yeah, and now I have this muscle thing. I have the worst luck," Bryan said.

They reached the change room.

"How do you feel?" Bryan asked tentatively.

"Okay. I've never run in a track meet before ..." Lionel reached for the door.

Bryan stopped him from going in. "Normal to be a bit nervous, even I'm nervous a bit and I've been in tons of meets." He looked off down the hallway. "Since we're both running in the fifteen hundred, maybe we should have a strategy, like work together, pace each other."

"I guess," Lionel said.

He didn't get it. How were they going to work together in a race — piggyback?

"Awesome," Bryan said. "We'll stay with the pack for the first couple of laps, and then push it hard in lap three. We can take turns running in front, cutting the wind for each other. We call it drafting. You've seen that, right? We can conserve energy for the big kick on the final lap. Don't go out too fast, though. That's a classic rookie error. You'll burn yourself out and have nothing for your kick. Make sense?"

"Yeah, sure," Lionel said.

Bryan patted him on the back. "You'll be fine. I've been watching you in pratise. You can run."

"The Green Machine is about to make his big, fat track debut."

Lionel's heart began to beat faster — Nick!

"Do you have a transporter machine?" Bryan said.

Bryan sounded nervous.

"Told Whellan I had to pee," Nick said.

Lionel reached for the door.

"What's the hurry?" Nick asked. He grabbed Lionel by the shoulder and spun him away from the door.

"I don't get disrespected by losers," Nick said, "and that means you."

"I didn't disrespect you," Lionel said.

Nick laughed. "Check him out. He admits he's a loser."

"We got a track meet ..." Bryan said, his voice shaky.

"We should break his legs then," Nick said.

Bryan looked bewildered. "We gotta get dressed, Nick. I need to warm up ... my pulled muscle."

"I've got to get dressed too," Lionel said.

Nick pushed Lionel backwards.

"Bad-mouth me to Kiana? You're dead," Nick snarled.

Nick straight-armed Lionel in the chest and then side-kicked his thigh.

"I'm going to rip your tongue out, you fat, ugly, stupid blabber-mouth," Nick said, his fists clenched, face purple with rage.

"I didn't say anything to her," Lionel said.

"Sorry, loser. She told me. You blabbed to her about the bet."

"I asked her if there was a bet and she said no."

Nick kicked him in the leg again.

"Did I ask you?" Nick thundered. His face turned even darker. "You're going to tell her you made it all up to make me look bad."

"I ..."

"Shut up," Nick said.

He punched Lionel in the ribs. Lionel gasped and he stepped back.

"This is stupid, Nick," Bryan said. "We got a meet ..."

"Shut up or I'll rip your face off too," Nick said. He turned back to Lionel. "As for you, you're going to tell her you made the whole story up because ... you're jealous of me ... or whatever. I don't care. She thinks I'm a weasel because of you."

"All I did was tell her the truth," Lionel said.

Nick slapped his face. "No kidding, dummy, and for some reason she thinks that makes me a bad person. So tell her it's not true."

Nick punched Lionel in the stomach.

It didn't hurt. The kicks and the slap hadn't either. Lionel had always been terrified of getting hit. He'd never actually been hit, though, not since his father used to whack him around. But that was a long time ago — and he wasn't the same Lionel.

"Are you hearing me?" Nick said.

Lionel wasn't really listening. He was thinking about his dad. He remembered how scared he used to be after a baseball game, especially if he struck out or messed up a play. He used to be so scared he wouldn't want to get in the car to go home. His dad used to hit him all the time.

Lionel looked up at Nick. He wasn't going to lie to Kiana out of fear — and he sure wasn't going to let Nick beat him up because his dad was a jerk.

Nick charged. Lionel swung his right hand and caught Nick on the side of the head. Nick jabbed with his left. Lionel shifted to his right to avoid the blow and hit Nick in the side with another right. Nick threw a wild right hand. Lionel ducked and drove his fist into his side again, and followed it up with a left jab to the top of Nick's head. Nick roared and jumped at Lionel with his arms extended.

The next second Nick lay on the floor.

"Freakin' idiot," Nick sputtered.

Bryan had body-checked him with his shoulder. He stood next to Lionel, breathing heavily.

Lionel felt a rush of exhilaration.

Nick got up slowly, his fists clenched. "Two on one? Freakin' losers."

Nick straightened up and pushed out his chest. He didn't look the same to Lionel, though. He looked like any other kid, nothing special, and Lionel wondered why he'd ever thought Nick was so scary.

"This ain't over," Nick said.

"I think it is," Lionel said.

"See ya around, Nick," Bryan said. "I've had enough of you too. So has Mohamed. Go ask him."

"Who cares?" Nick said.

"Let's get changed," Lionel said to Bryan.

He opened the door and Bryan went in.

"Tough guy is running away," Nick called out.

Lionel let the door close behind him.

"Big, fat, smelly loser," Nick yelled. "I'm gonna kick your ass."

Lionel went to an open spot and began to dress.

A few minutes later, Whellan walked in. "Let's hurry up, boys," he said. "The junior events start in about thirty minutes. Seniors, you have a bit of a wait, but I still want everyone to warm up together. So if you're dressed, get out on the track."

Most of the boys got up and began filing out. Whellan came over and sat next to Lionel.

"How're you feeling, Lionel?"

"Good."

He ran his hand over his chin. "I've been thinking of your race, Lionel. I want you to set a very fast pace from the start. Make it very uncomfortable for everyone to keep up. No free rides. Push it hard, and at the very least stay up with the leaders. By the second lap, most of the kids will be too tired to have much of a kick. If you have more in the tank, I want you to run harder. Keep pushing yourself. I think you have reserves you haven't even tested yet."

"We were going to pace each other," Bryan said. His face was paler than normal.

"Bryan, do your best and try to get in the top ten." Whellan pointed at Lionel. "After two laps, you take off no matter what. Show me what you can do. Okay?"

Lionel nodded.

"But I kinda thought we should run together," Bryan said.

"Don't worry about Lionel," Whellan said. "You run your own race."

Bryan seemed about to say something, but then he nodded and looked down.

"You run your own race, too," Whellan said forcefully to Lionel.

"I'll try," Lionel said.

"Awesome." He stood up. "Let's have everyone out on the track in fifteen minutes for a group warm up," Whellan said loudly.

He left. "You can win this race," Bryan said to Lionel in a quiet voice. "You're the fastest long-distance kid in school. Whellan's right. You go for it. Don't worry about me."

Lionel had a feeling he was more worried about Nick than the race. "There's only one Nick and there are a bunch of us who've had enough of him, Stephane ... Jaime. We stick together, there's no problem."

"You're right."

"And thanks ... for helping me with Nick back there."

"You didn't need it."

"Nice to have the help anyway."

Bryan grinned sheepishly and held out a fist. Lionel gave it a punch. They both finished changing, neither feeling the need to say any more about it.

Lionel wasn't worried about Nick, but was a little nervous about the race. It was one thing to run in the street, and something completely different to run in a track meet in front of the entire school.

It suddenly occurred to him that even after the fight, and even though he was about to run in his first track meet, he felt pretty good — no headache and his chest wasn't tight.

Maybe he could throw those pills out soon?

## Monday: 2:30 p.m.

A huge cheer went up. A girl in a blue uniform threw her hands in the air as she crossed the finish line, followed closely by two others. Lionel searched for Kiana in the crowd of runners waiting for the second heat of the eight-hundred-meter race. He couldn't see her.

"Yo, Lionel."

A hand clapped him on the back.

"Deepak? Afonso?"

"You thought we were gonna miss this?" Deepak grinned. He elbowed Afonso. "We both have dentist appointments — apparently."

Lionel let himself laugh. He needed to. His nerves were kicking up. The boys' senior fifteen hundred was soon.

"You feel loose, strong, powerful, stoked, mean — and angry?" Deepak said.

"I think I'm loose," Lionel said.

They laughed, which relaxed him even more. He noticed Afonso had a big bag with him.

"What's that?"

"My camera," Afonso said. "I'm going to capture the magic."

"Shouldn't we start with fifty mega close-ups of me?" Deepak said.

"The lens will crack. Can't get too close to that face," Afonso said.

"Photography is so complicated," Deepak said.

"Kiana's race is about to start," Lionel said. "You should get the camera out."

He'd love to have a picture of Kiana running. It would be creepy to ask, obviously.

"I'll snap a few for you," Afonso said.

He didn't seem to care.

"Thanks," Lionel said.

Deepak cupped his hands around his mouth. "Go, Kiana, go. Go, Kiana, go."

"There's Gwen," Afonso pointed.

Gwen and Binny came running over.

"Did we miss her?" she said, out of breath.

"Just about to start," Deepak said.

"You're so lucky," Gwen said to Binny.

"More exciting this way," Binny grinned.

"Binny had to do a million things this morning. I think I liked you better when you were lazy," Gwen said, laughing.

The runners took their places at the starting line. The starter held a pistol over her head. It went off and the girls charged forward.

"C'mon Kiana," Deepak cried.

"Let's go, baby," Gwen said quietly.

They rounded the first corner and then converged into a pack midway through the back straightaway.

Afonso snapped a couple of pics.

"Kiana's making her move," Gwen said excitedly.

She'd shifted outside and passed a few girls, falling in behind the leader, about two yards back.

"Excuse me," Lionel heard a woman say.

Kiana and the first place girl pulled farther ahead on the rest of the pack as they headed into the front straightaway. They flew along the track and into the second lap.

"Excuse me. Thanks."

Afonso moved over.

"Lionel, dear. I haven't missed your race, have I?"

"Mom? What are you doing here?" Lionel said.

She tilted her head to the side. "I'm here to see your race," she said.

"Um, sure ... but work?"

"I mentioned to Sheila that you were in a track meet and she went all crazy and told me I had to come." She laughed quietly. "Anyway, I hurried over and ... here I am."

Kiana tried to pass the girl on the back straightaway, but

she wouldn't let her get in front. The crowd began to cheer louder.

"C'mon, Kiana. C'mon," Gwen said urgently. "This is the same girl who beat her in the Citys. She has a massive kick. Kiana needs to push now."

"Is that Kiana … the girl with the braids?" his mom whispered to Lionel.

"Yes, Mom," Lionel said.

The two girls pulled farther away and headed into the final lap.

"Go Kiana," Deepak yelled. He was jumping up and down.

Afonso's camera clicked away.

The girls headed into the final straightaway. Kiana was still behind.

"Now, Kiana," Lionel yelled. "Go!"

The gap between them opened slightly, then a touch more, then even wider. Lionel lowered his chin and he stomped his foot on the ground. Kiana was going to come second.

"That girl's gotten into Kiana's head," Gwen said.

They crossed the finish line. The girl threw her hands over her head. Kiana slowed and put her hands on her hips.

"Second is pretty good," Deepak said.

"Maybe," Gwen said. "They have one more heat, but I think that one will be the fastest. Kiana's not going to be a happy camper, though. She really wanted to win."

Sure enough, when Kiana came over, her eyes were flashing angrily.

"I choked," she said to Gwen. "I tightened up and did every-thing wrong."

Gwen rubbed the back of Kiana's head gently. "That's why we race," she said. "Learn from your mistakes. You didn't go out hard enough and she had too much in reserve. You're stronger than her, but not in the last hundred."

"Then why didn't I do it?" Kiana fumed. She kicked at a rock on the ground.

Gwen laughed. "You tell me."

"'Cause I'm stupid?" Kiana said.

"That was my guess," Deepak said.

Kiana dropped her shoulders. "You're supposed to be supportive — and in school. What's up?"

"We have a dentist appointment ... or a doctor appointment ... or ..." Deepak looked at Afonso. "What do we have?"

"A burning desire to see a track meet?" Afonso said.

Binny laughed outright. Gwen tried not to.

"You boys are so bad," Gwen said. "I'm a responsible adult and I know your parents."

Deepak turned to Lionel. "This may be a very obvious attempt at changing the subject, but ... is this your famous mom?"

Lionel felt himself blushing furiously. "Yeah. Sorry. Mom, these are the guys I run with, the Marketeers: Deepak, Afonso; you've met Kiana's mom, Gwen, and her dad, Binny — and that's Kiana."

"Hi, I'm Charlene."

"The boys' senior fifteen hundred meter is next. Please come to the starting area," a voice called out on the loudspeaker.

"You've got this, Lionel," Deepak said.

Afonso clicked a picture. "I want a before-shot of the winner."

"Good luck," Charlene said.

Kiana stood in front of him and took his hand. "You are going to win this race," she said.

He felt ridiculous.

"Say it," she said.

"I'm going to ... win this race."

"Like you mean it," Kiana said.

"C'mon. This is dumb."

"Say it," she said intensely.

She seemed deadly serious. No one else was laughing, either.

"You have to believe you can do it," Kiana said. "We all know you can. You're the only one who doesn't. Now say it."

A rush of energy surged through his body. "I'm going to win this race," he said.

They all cheered.

He looked at them. They were so important to him it was hard to express. Obviously, his mom was ... well ... his mom, and she'd become a real mom lately. Deepak and Afonso — they were friends, good friends, and why shouldn't he accept that? Why couldn't he have friends? They'd come to see Kiana run, but him too. Gwen and Binny were great. They were older, but they were fun to be with. They made him feel good about himself.

Kiana?

Enough said. She was perfect.

But what if he sucked and came last? Kiana would lose respect for him and ...

"You probably need to actually run in the race, if you're going to win," Deepak said, pushing him towards the track.

Lionel wanted to say something to them. How much it meant to him that they were here.

"I don't care what place you come in," Kiana said. "Just don't lose because you think you can't win."

Her words hit him like a hammer.

"Last call for the boys' fifteen hundred," the voice blared.

"Go," Kiana said.

Lionel ran to the starting area, his heart racing, his mind in a whirl.

*Don't lose because you think you can't win.*

Could he win? He wanted to so badly it hurt, to make Kiana proud, and his mom. Everyone.

The woman with the starter pistol was talking to the runners.

"We're only running one heat," she said. "There are sixteen runners, so be careful at the start. I'm sure you've all run this distance lots of times, but I'm supposed to tell you that it's three full laps and then the last lap is only three-quarters of the way around."

"That's way too far," someone joked.

The boys laughed.

Lionel looked at the track. Almost four laps. It was a long race.

Bryan pulled him aside. "Whellan asked me not to tell you, but we're tied with Brockton, Hamadi Kalu's school. This is the last race of the meet. Whoever gets the most points in this race could win it. Brockton only has one kid in this race, Kalu, so if you win, we win.

"But if you and I get more than ten points between us …"

"I'm not going to be in the top ten. No chance."

"Is your leg that bad?"

Bryan looked off for a moment. "My leg's fine. I'm … I'm just not in your league. It's up to you." He crossed his arms and kicked at the track. "And sorry for all the stuff I did. I was a jerk and … I'm sorry."

"Don't be saying sorry," Lionel said. "Listen, I need your help to win this thing. Go out as hard as you can in the first lap and I'll run right behind you — drafting — like you said. That'll let me keep more energy for the big kick against Kalu."

Bryan stood up taller and he nodded. "No problem. Let's do this."

He held out his fist and they punched.

"Please line up," the starter said.

Most of the boys dashed for a spot close to the inside. Kiana, Deepak, and Afonso were at the start line. Whellan was standing behind them. Kids and parents lined the track practically the entire length of the straightaway. He even saw Mohamed!

A cold sweat broke out all over him. If he didn't beat this Kalu kid, Brockton was through to the regionals. He'd have messed up in front of the whole school.

The starter laughed. "No killing each other before the race. You still have fifteen hundred meters to go."

The boys were jostling for position. Lionel lined up on the outside behind another runner.

"Back off, goof," Lionel heard Bryan say to another kid.

Bryan leaned into him.

"Then move over, jerk," the boy said.

"Bite me," Bryan said.

"Everyone needs to calm down," a third boy said. "It's not like any of you can beat me."

"You can bite me, too, Kalu," Bryan said.

Kalu laughed. "I'm sorry, did you win the Citys last year?"

"You're living in the past, bro," Bryan said. "You're about to be introduced to second place." He looked over at Lionel and winked.

Lionel took a moment to check Kalu out. He was rail thin and not very tall. Lionel touched his own stomach instinctively. His pot belly was gone.

He'd always thought of himself as a fat kid.

But he wasn't anymore.

The guys were beginning to act like this was a football game, jamming elbows into ribs, and pushing guys away with their arms.

"All you, Lionel. No problem," Deepak yelled.

His mom waved to him.

"You got a fan club?" a boy in front of Lionel said.

"No. It's just … friends and …"

"Is that your mommy in case you fall and get a boo-boo?" he said.

"What's with the clown shoes?" another kid said. "You lose a bet?"

Lionel's mind raced.

"Good comeback, bro," the boy in front said, laughing.

Lionel bent his knees and got ready. He'd sound like an idiot no matter what he said. Bryan was still chirping with Kalu and things were almost out of control, with guys pushing and shoving and trash talking, when suddenly the starter raised the pistol in the air.

"Runners take your marks, get set …"

The gun fired.

The boys surged.

Lionel looked around. Didn't she have to say go?

"Run!" Kiana screamed.

He took off like a shot. Stupid idiot. Already in last place. He was supposed to be right behind Bryan. He sprinted all out. By the end of the first corner, he'd pulled even with the back of the pack. Lionel slowed his pace. Up ahead, about ten yards, four runners had formed a leader pack, including Hamadi Kalu.

Lionel spotted Bryan. He shifted outside and ran up to him.

"Where were you?" Bryan said.

He was panting heavily.

"I got a bad start," Lionel said.

"Let's get you to the front," Bryan said.

"Right behind you," Lionel said.

They entered the second corner.

Bryan began to sprint. Lionel hung off his shoulder and followed along. It really was easier to run behind someone. There was a bit of a headwind and he didn't even feel it.

He looked at Bryan. His lips were tight and his face strained. His head was bobbing up and down.

The leaders rounded the corner and headed up the front straightaway.

"Go for it," Bryan gasped. "I'm done."

Lionel charged after them. He crossed the spot where Bryan had tripped him. Back then he'd given up and let himself fall.

He wasn't the same Lionel.

He had friends.

He had a wonderful mom — who loved him.

He'd stood up to Nick — and he would help Stephane and Jaime.

And ... he had a beautiful girlfriend named Kiana who only wanted him to run his best.

Lionel caught the leaders by the start line.

"Do you guys always run this slow?" Lionel said.

"I don't see you in front, Green Shoes," Kalu said.

"That's the Green Machine to you, bro," Lionel said.

The boys burst out laughing — until Lionel exploded past them.

The crowd cheered him on as he blasted into the first corner of lap two. He looked over his right shoulder. Kalu was still with him. The other three runners were already five yards behind, and falling back fast.

"You're serious about this?" Kalu said.

Lionel could see him shift outside. He was going to try and pass. Lionel lengthened his stride and went faster. Whellan had said he should push it. Kiana said he didn't get tired. Time to find out if they were right.

"This will be fun," Kalu said. "Show me what you got."

Lionel continued to lead for the next lap. They ran together, stride for stride, Kalu seemingly content to let him stay in front. They came into the front straightaway.

"I should thank you for letting me draft off you. Cuts the wind nicely, thank you," Kalu said.

Stephane, Jaime, and Angelina were standing by the edge of the track.

"Last lap. You're doing great," Stephane called out.

Angelina and Jaime were jumping up and down.

"Take it home, bro!" Mohamed yelled.

"You have a lot of fans," Kalu said. "Hope they enjoy seeing me — and Brockton — win."

Kalu spurted forward. Lionel responded by speeding up himself. They raced up the straightaway — three-quarters of a lap to go.

The bell rang.

Kiana was clapping over her head and yelling. Afonso was taking pictures. Deepak and Binny were doing a crazy dance of some sort. Gwen and his mom were cheering him on.

Kalu dropped in behind Lionel.

"You can run into the wind again," Kalu gasped. He was breathing heavily.

Lionel didn't feel much of a wind. He entered the corner and pressed on. The curve let him take a glance inside. It was a two-man race. The nearest runners were twenty yards back, and the main pack wasn't even close.

Lionel let his body take over. He lengthened his stride even longer and swung his arms from his shoulders. He could go faster. Lionel gritted his teeth and pushed himself. He came out of the final corner. He couldn't hear Kalu behind him. He was running alone, but he didn't feel alone.

Kiana had given him all the advice he ever needed, the one word that had changed his life.

Run!